# MEET THE FORTUNES!

**Fortune of the Month:** Austin Fortune

**Age:** 33

**Vital Statistics:** Tall, dark and handsome—some might say *intense*. One of the New Orleans Fortunes, Austin is a *very* eligible bachelor.

**Claim to Fame:** He's an investment banker with baggage. Money has not brought him happiness.

**Romantic Prospects:** His first marriage was a disaster, and he's determined not to make the same mistake twice. Even if the perfect woman is standing right in front of him.

"Some people are just not cut out to be married. I *am* married—to my job. I don't need a wife. I have Felicity, the world's most efficient assistant. At least for now. She has told me that she is leaving me, that is, leaving Fortune Investments. Suddenly I'm in a panic.

"It's funny. Ever since Felicity gave her notice, I can't stop thinking about her. But a personal involvement is out of the question. I don't *do* personal. And I'm her boss! There has to be another way to convince her to stay..."

\* \* \*

**THE FORTUNES OF TEXAS:
THE LOST FORTUNES—
Family secrets revealed!**

Dear Reader,

Have you ever wanted something that seemed out of your reach?

Felicity Schafer, the heroine of *A Fortunate Arrangement*, fell in love with Austin Fortune the moment she laid eyes on him. The only problem... he was her boss. To compound matters, he was part of the illustrious Fortune family and ran in social circles that left her feeling as if she was on the outside looking in. Then a funny thing happened. A series of events made her realize that she was in charge of her destiny. If she wanted more, first, she had to believe herself worthy. There's nothing like a confident woman to make a man sit up and take notice...

I hope you enjoy Felicity and Austin's story as much as I enjoyed writing it. Please join me at Facebook.com/nrobardsthompson, Instagram.com/nancyrthompson/ and Twitter.com/nrtwrites, or drop me a line at nrobardsthompson@yahoo.com. I love to hear from readers!

Warmly,

*Nancy*

# A Fortunate Arrangement

*Nancy Robards Thompson*

Special thanks and acknowledgment to Nancy Robards Thompson for her contribution to the Fortunes of Texas: The Lost Fortunes continuity.

Recycling programs
for this product may
not exist in your area.

ISBN-13: 978-1-335-57382-7

A Fortunate Arrangement

Copyright © 2019 by Harlequin Books S.A.

**Printed in U.S.A.**

HARLEQUIN®
www.Harlequin.com

National bestselling author **Nancy Robards Thompson** holds a degree in journalism. She worked as a newspaper reporter until she realized reporting "just the facts" bored her silly. Now that she has much more content to report to her muse, Nancy loves writing women's fiction and romance full-time. Critics have deemed her work "funny, smart and observant." She resides in Florida with her husband and daughter. You can reach her at Facebook.com/nrobardsthompson.

## Books by Nancy Robards Thompson

### Harlequin Special Edition

#### Celebration, TX

*The Cowboy's Runaway Bride*
*A Bride, a Barn, and a Baby*
*The Cowboy Who Got Away*

#### Celebrations, Inc.

*Texas Wedding*
*Texas Magic*
*Texas Christmas*

#### The Fortunes of Texas: Rulebreakers

*Maddie Fortune's Perfect Man*

#### The Fortunes of Texas: The Secret Fortunes

*Fortune's Surprise Engagement*

#### The Fortunes of Texas: All Fortune's Children

*Fortune's Prince Charming*

#### The Fortunes of Texas: Cowboy Country

*My Fair Fortune*

Visit the Author Profile page
at Harlequin.com for more titles.

This book is dedicated to the "Hey, Tinas," who are living proof that friendship can thrive despite the miles and mountains between us.

## Chapter One

Austin Fortune almost missed the plain white envelope at the bottom of the stack of papers his assistant Felicity Schafer had set on his desk. After he'd read the letter, he wished he'd never seen it and for a moment, he considered pretending as if he hadn't read it.

Maybe it would just disappear.

Instead, the reality of it danced around him like illuminated dust motes.

Felicity, his gatekeeper, his right hand, the person who kept him organized and on track ahead of the fray, had tendered her resignation.

"Is this a bad joke?" he muttered aloud, trying it on for size.

But no. Even though Felicity was good-natured, it

would've been out of character for her to kid around about something like this.

"She's leaving me." Uttering the words out loud made it sound personal. It wasn't personal—it was work, but it sure felt personal.

He looked up from the note and watched her through the glass wall of his office. She was engrossed in something on her computer. He didn't know what. He could see her in profile. Her head was bowed over her keyboard, her dark blond hair a curtain hiding her face.

What the hell was he supposed to do without her? Every morning when he got to the office, she had a daily briefing typed up and waiting for him on his desk along with his coffee and a smoothie with energy booster. She remembered birthdays, anniversaries and the minutiae of family and client particulars that elevated and solidified his business relationships and could prove costly if forgotten. She was always game for brainstorming new concepts and abstract business angles. Ultimately assisting with client presentations.

Plain and simple, Felicity made him look good and was always there to help him succeed.

It wasn't just a matter of hiring someone new. Felicity was a rare find. She had an uncanny ability to anticipate his every need—even before he knew what he needed. In all fairness, he paid her well and she seemed happy. So, why was she leaving him?

He skimmed the letter again looking for clues, but in true Felicity form, it was short and to the point:

Dear Austin,

Please accept this letter as notification that I am leaving my position with Fortune Investments at the end of the month.

I've left the date open, so I can be of assistance during the transition.

Sincerely,

Felicity Schafer

Austin reread the note twice more, making sure he'd read it right. Once he'd absorbed it, he had a good idea of how he might fix it. He pressed the button on the intercom.

"Felicity, could you come into my office, please?"

"Sure."

A moment later, she was standing in his doorway.

"What do you need?" she asked.

"If you wanted a raise," he said, "all you had to do was ask."

She wrinkled her nose. "A raise?"

"Of course, you just had your half-year review and got a bump in salary, but if it wasn't enough, if you want more money, we can talk about it."

She gave her head a quick shake. "Who said anything about a raise?"

He picked up her letter. "I thought maybe that's what this was about. I mean why else would you resign?"

Her cheeks flushed, and her mouth fell open before she snapped it shut, into a thin line and folded her arms across her chest. She looked at him as if he had insulted her.

*How could offering someone more money be insulting?*

He leaned back in his chair, crossing his arms, mirroring her posture.

"Austin, you've always been generous when it comes to my salary. But I'm graduating with my MBA at the end of the month. I don't need a graduate degree to be someone's personal assistant. It's time I moved on."

"Do you have another job?"

"No, not yet. I'm going to start interviewing soon. I wanted to be up-front with you about it."

"Thanks," he said.

She flinched. He realized he might have sounded sarcastic. Maybe a very small part of him had meant it that way. Was he supposed to be happy he was losing her?

He raked his hand through his hair. This was not the way he wanted to start his Friday. It certainly wasn't the way he wanted to end his week.

He gestured for her to sit down in one of the chairs on the other side of his desk.

She sat and folded her hands in her lap. "I've loved working for you and Fortune Investments, but I've worked hard to get this degree."

He didn't say anything because he was afraid what he wanted to say would sound wrong. He'd always prided himself on being fair.

"I hope you can understand that I want more than being someone's secretary for the rest of my working life," she went on. "Because that's what I am. We can dress it up and call me your assistant, but when it comes down to it, I'm your secretary. It's been a great job, but now I need more."

He held up his hand.

"I get it," he said. "I do. Congratulations on accomplishing this, Felicity. I'm happy for you. I know how hard you've worked. You're smart and you're creative and I understand that a person with an MBA is way overqualified to be a personal assistant. You'd be wasting your potential staying in this position. But that doesn't make it any easier for me because I don't want to lose you."

He held her gaze and her expression softened.

"I mean did you expect me not to be upset about the prospect of losing you?" He held up his hand again to signal that the question was rhetorical. "But that's me being selfish. This isn't about me. It's about you. What do you want to do with your degree?"

"My undergraduate degree is in advertising. I've always wanted to work in that field."

"You'd be good at it," he said. "You'd be good at anything you decided to do."

Her cheeks turned pink again. She looked down and then back up at him.

"Is there anything I can do to convince you to stay with Fortune Investments?"

"I don't know. Are there any opportunities here?"

"What if I talk to Miles and see if we can create a position for you? I'm not making any promises, but would you consider staying if we could come up with something?"

Felicity smiled. "It depends. Would it mean doing advertising work in addition to everything I do for you?"

Austin laughed. "You know me too well."

"I know I do."

"How am I supposed to get by without you, Felicity?"

She shrugged. "You did fine before I came on board. You'll survive."

No, he hadn't been fine before she came onto the scene. His life had been a mess, a big tumbleweed of mistakes and misjudgments that had cost him dearly. It had taken him five years to get himself back on track after his disastrous marriage. Sure, he'd come through it intact and he'd learned a lot about himself and life. Yes, he would be fine on his own, but he didn't want to lose her.

"If they can't create a position for me, I'd like to stay until after graduation, and as I said in my letter, I'll stay until we find my replacement."

Maybe if he didn't find someone new, she wouldn't go. It would be like waiting for tomorrow. Did tomorrow ever really come?

"I'll tell you what. I'm having dinner with Miles tonight. I'll broach the subject with him and let you know what he says. Sound good? You won't quit on me before you let me figure something out, right?"

*How am I supposed to get by without you, Felicity?*

If she was a silly woman, Felicity would've let herself read so much into that question. But true to form, she had already overthought it, turning it round and round in her mind, examining it from every angle until it had completely lost its shape and she'd killed off any dreams that Austin Fortune felt anything for her that wasn't strictly platonic.

However, her heart hadn't gotten the memo from her brain, because her heart thudded in her chest like a drum in a New Orleans funeral procession.

He'd said *get by*.

He didn't say *live without you*.

There was a world of difference between the statements. Like night and day. Love and like. Get by and live without.

Even so, she couldn't shake the satisfaction she felt over his reaction to her letter of resignation. Sure, she'd known he wouldn't be happy, but she hadn't fathomed that he would react the way he did.

She stole a glance at Austin through the glass wall that separated his office from her workspace. He was wearing that blue button-down that she liked so much. It contrasted with his dark hair and those soulful brown eyes. Eyes that hypnotized her, that made her lose track of time and occasionally space out and miss what he was saying because she'd been totally transported.

Her thudding heart slowed, leaving her more breathless and full of longing.

*He acted like I was breaking up with him.*

*As if I'd ever break up with him.*

*If I ever had him.*

*But I never will.*

Why did she have to be in love with her boss?

Why did he have to dangle the potential of a promotion in front of her? She thought she wanted a clean break, so she could get on with her life and forget about him and this ridiculous crush, but the moment he'd offered to talk to his father, all fresh starts flew out the window.

Of course, the Fortunes had been so good to her. They were dream employers. The pay and benefits were top-notch. The working conditions were first class.

She stole another glance at Austin and her ridiculous heart picked up the cadence right where it had left off.

Felicity knew she shouldn't get her hopes up. Fortune Investments was a family firm. Austin's sister Georgia handled public relations for the investment firm. They'd never had to advertise in the true sense of the word—not the kind of advertising Felicity wanted to do. They'd built their business on solid reputation and word of mouth. But even from her position as support staff, she knew the business had grown.

Maybe they were ready to expand.

If she got a promotion, it was likely that she'd be in a different department with a different supervisor. Which would mean Austin wouldn't be her boss anymore—

*Don't even go there.*

She'd worked with him for almost five years and during that time, it had been all business all the time. What made her think anything would change if she got promoted?

*Yeah, well, a girl can dream.*

Just not on Fortune Investments' time.

"Did you do it?" Maia Fredericks asked after she let herself in Felicity's patio door. She didn't knock. Maia never knocked. Felicity didn't mind because her friend's hands were never empty when she came over. This evening, she was carrying a bottle of something that looked like it could be champagne.

"I did," Felicity said.

"Well, how did it go? Don't keep me waiting." Maia dislodged the cork on the bottle. Felicity winced at the loud popping sound.

"You do know you're not supposed to open champagne that way, right? Besides the possibility of damaging eardrums and putting out someone's eye, it kills the bubbles and the taste."

"This way is more fun," Maia said, helping herself to two flutes from Felicity's china cabinet. "Besides, it's not champagne. It's sparkling rosé."

"Same principle," Felicity said. "Haven't you heard the saying, *the ear's gain is the palate's loss*?"

Maia made a face and waved away her words with a flippant flick of her hand. "You gave your notice. We're celebrating, and I wanted to start the night off with a bang. How did he take the news?"

Felicity shrugged. "He took it about as well as you might expect."

Maia handed Felicity a glass of sparkling rosé.

Felicity couldn't suppress a smile thinking about how upset he'd been by the news.

*How am I supposed to get by without you, Felicity?*

Did she dare tell Maia what he said? One of two things would happen: her friend would either point out what Felicity already knew—it wasn't personal. It simply meant that she was good at her job. Or she would read way too much into it and try to tempt Felicity into abandoning her common sense about where she stood with Austin Fortune.

Either way, this little nugget was best kept bottled up. Because much like the sparkling wine Maia had brought over to help her celebrate, once the feeling was uncorked, it wouldn't be long before the harsh reality made it flat and unpalatable.

Actually, that was Felicity's view on romance in general. Once romance was set in motion, it was as if a clock started ticking, counting down toward the inevitable end.

Instead of letting the air out of her giddy feeling, she sipped her drink and closed her eyes, savoring the bubbles that tickled her nose.

"What exactly does that mean?" Maia asked. "The guy has his good days and he has his beastly days. Which was this? Was he Mr. Wonderful or was he the Beast?"

Maia knew way too much about Felicity's unrequited crush on her boss. The two women were next-door neighbors, each owning half of a double shotgun-style home that had been converted into two units. They had become fast friends that cool February evening when Felicity moved in and Maia, bearing a casserole of red beans and rice and a bottle of zinfandel, had knocked on Felicity's door and introduced herself.

Felicity had invited her in and amid a maze of boxes, they'd bonded as they feasted on the dinner and wine.

Four years later, they shared more than a common interior wall and communal outdoor space. Maia was so easy to talk to that Felicity constantly found herself confiding secrets that in the past she would've never entrusted to anyone. Secrets such as the big honking crush she'd had on Austin since the day he'd hired her.

"Austin was…Austin." She shrugged. "He was all business, as usual."

Maia didn't just frown, she looked outraged. "What? He just said okay and was fine with letting you walk out of his life forever?"

"I gave my notice. I didn't ask him for a divorce."

"I know that," Maia said. "Did he not show any emotion at all?"

"He didn't cry, if that's what you were expecting."

"Don't be ridiculous. Of course he wouldn't cry. Beasts don't cry. But they do bellow. Did he bellow? Please tell me at the very least he bellowed. If he didn't, I'll have to worry about him."

"You're ridiculous," Felicity said.

Truly, she was. Ridiculously good at getting Felicity to spill her guts. Because suddenly, she was brimming over with the need to tell Maia everything.

"He said he didn't want me to go." Felicity bit her bottom lip. Maia looked at her expectantly. "Actually, he said, 'How am I supposed to get by without you?'"

"Oooh, giiirl." Maia whistled.

And that was how Maia did it. It was *that* subtle, almost like sleight of hand. One minute, Felicity would be steadfast in her resolution to bury a secret deep in her heart, in a place only she knew. Then somehow Maia had diverted her attention and extracted the secret from her.

"*Get by* without you," Felicity repeated. "Not *live*

without you. There's a world of difference in *getting by* and *living*."

Maia shook her head. "Same thing, baby girl. That's simply Beast-speak. He loves you. You need to tell him how you feel."

This time Felicity was the one shaking her head.

"Then you're telling me *you're* perfectly happy *getting by* rather than *living*?" The woman was relentless. "But he let you off work early." Maia glanced at her watch. "Relatively speaking. It's 6:45. I guess that's almost normal business hours."

"He's having dinner with his parents tonight," Felicity said. "After that, he's catching a flight to Atlanta for a meeting tomorrow. I was at a good stopping point. I figured it wouldn't hurt to call it a day at a reasonable hour for a change."

"I'm surprised he didn't insist that you go to Atlanta with him. Seems like he has a hard time functioning without you there to keep everything in order."

Felicity would've loved to go to Atlanta with him. Arriving at the hotel, which would allow her to indulge in the brief illusion that they were checking in together. One room. A king-size bed. Both of them naked, spending one glorious night making love—

Felicity tried to shake the image of hot, sweaty, naked Austin. It wasn't the first time she'd thought about what he'd look like naked. She just knew that underneath his custom fit Tom Ford suits, Austin's body would be long and lean and sexy. His shoulders—oh, those shoulders, they were so perfect they made her want to weep— those broad shoulders would give way to strong, muscled arms—not too muscled, but just right so that his biceps would bulge when he pulled her into his arms and against his perfectly defined chest. Lean hips would showcase a washboard-flat stomach just above the part of his body that would rock her world.

She drew in a sharp breath. She couldn't help it. That's what he did to her. It wasn't considered objectifying a man if you were in love with him, right? She didn't think of anyone else like this. She didn't want to just sleep with him—okay, she did want to sleep with him and she'd fully imagined that experience, too. She wanted so much more than lust or a one-night stand. She wanted to love Austin and she wanted him to love her, too. But he didn't. Clearly, he didn't.

Her sexy daydreams were the consolation prize for the fact that beyond the office, Austin didn't even realize she existed.

"That's not true," Felicity said, answering her friend's comment about how Austin couldn't function without her.

Maia pinned her with a dubious look.

"Okay, maybe it's partially true," Felicity conceded. "It's called job security. I make myself indispensable and I keep getting paid."

"I think you're long past needing to worry about job security. How long has it been now?"

"Almost five years."

"Do you think he will remember your anniversary?" There was a gleam in Maia's eye that Felicity tried to ignore. "I think it's an occasion that calls for flowers and jewelry."

"Stop. He's my boss. There will be no jewelry involved. Because I'll be at my new job by then."

"But you wouldn't mind jewelry. Maybe a ring?"

"Maia, stop. Even if I was still working there, I doubt it would even cross his mind to get me a card. I'm sure in his mind my paycheck is proof of his appreciation."

Austin did pay her well. She couldn't dispute that. Once, when she'd been offered an entry-level position as an account executive with a local advertising agency, she'd given him two weeks' notice. He'd doubled her salary without blinking an eye.

He'd told her she was worth it.

For a bright and shiny moment, she'd read something deeper into his words. Something that bordered on personal. Then she'd blinked and the next thing she knew, he'd launched into what a hassle it would be to find and train someone new and what an imposition it would be to suffer through a new assistant's initial learning curve.

The explanation had dulled the luster in a hurry.

Still, the money was nice. The raise had allowed her to save up a substantial down payment for a house. A year later she'd been in position to buy one of the units in the cute little green house in New Orleans's Irish Channel neighborhood. Technically, it was half a house, but it was hers and she loved it so much she wouldn't have traded it for one of the stately mansions in the neighboring Garden District. Well, in theory, anyway.

In the years she'd worked for Austin, nothing had changed. Felicity was still single, and Austin was none the wiser to her feelings for him. Every day was the same. Except, the days had morphed into weeks and weeks into months. Now, here she was looking back at nearly half a decade that had gone by in a heart-beat and she felt like a hamster on a wheel, bored and mostly unfulfilled by the sameness of it all, but safe and comfortable hiding behind her fat bank account and feelings for him she could never reveal.

Emotionally, she couldn't afford to go on like this much longer. She'd go insane. That's why she had promised herself she would quit and get a real job after she graduated with her MBA at the end of the month.

"I don't understand why you don't just level with him and tell him how you feel," Maia said. "You might just be surprised. I mean, you're leaving soon anyway. Nothing ventured, nothing gained."

Just the thought made Felicity want to turn and run. She had no idea where she wanted to run to other than somewhere far away from the idea of confessing her secret to Austin. In fact, right now she was sorry she'd confided in Maia. It wasn't the first time her friend had suggested such nonsense. She'd been bringing it up more frequently since Felicity had told her of her plans to leave after she graduated.

"Austin said tonight at dinner he would talk to his father about creating an advertising position for me. That's all the more reason why I need to keep my feel-ings to myself."

"I don't know," Maia mused. "Most likely, you won't be reporting to him anymore if they do make a posi-tion for you. Might be a good time to come clean with your feelings."

"Stop." Felicity held up her hand like a traffic cop. "Please listen to me. *If* they create a job for me—and that's a big *if*—I would be one of the few non-Fortunes in a position that wasn't support staff. If I start publicly mooning over Austin, it could be career suicide or at the very least I would embarrass myself."

Maia shrugged. "You look pretty cozy over there in your comfort zone."

"Leaving the comfort of a well-paying job is hardly staying in my comfort zone."

"You know what I'm talking about," Maia said. "I'm talking about the love part. I'm talking about you not wanting to put yourself out there. It was one thing to not want to jeopardize your job, but now that you're leaving you have no excuses."

Ah, but she did.

She hadn't shared it with Maia because her friend had never asked.

"You know what they say, a comfort zone is a very safe place, but nothing ever grows there—especially not love."

Felicity shook her head. "He has never given me any indication he feels the same way for me."

Maia sighed. "Fine. If you don't want to try to make things work with Austin, then you need to open your mind to other prospects."

"Such as?"

"Be open to dating other men."

Felicity sighed.

"I'm just saying," Maia said. "Just think about it. And since there's no use arguing with a brick wall, let's change the subject."

"Good."

"I have a huge favor to ask you," Maia said. "You know the hair show I'm doing next weekend?"

Felicity nodded.

"I've already sunk a boatload of money into this show and Jane Gordon, the girl who was going to be my model, got a paying modeling job in Paris. She had to bail on me."

"Oh, no. That's terrible. I'm sorry."

"It's good for her, but it stinks for me," Maia said. "So, I have an idea. Will you be my model?"

"Me?" Felicity laughed, unsure if Maia was joking. "I'm not a model."

Her friend set down her drink and walked over and started fluffing Felicity's hair and assessing her as if she was a horse at auction.

"If you try to pick up my leg and look at the bottom of my foot, I'm going to kick you," Felicity said. "I'm not a show pony. I don't do things like this."

"I'm not asking you to change careers." Maia smoothed Felicity's hair away from her face, shaping it into a high ponytail before she turned it loose and let it cascade around her shoulders. "Just help me out of this pickle."

## Chapter Two

Austin drove through the stately iron gates that surrounded his parents' rambling eight-bedroom, Garden District mansion. Miles and Sarah Fortune still lived in the same house where Austin and his six brothers and sisters had grown up. The sprawling Victorian was way too much house for most people, but maintaining the family home was a point of pride for them, especially on nights like this, when they called everyone together for a family dinner meeting.

Austin parked his Tesla next to his brother Beau's BMW. He took care to park where no one could block him in, since he'd have to leave early to catch a flight to Atlanta tonight.

He wound his way around the other cars that lined the driveway. When the family got together, it looked like Miles and Sarah were having a party. Tonight, it appeared that Austin was the last to arrive.

As he let himself in the front door, the antique grandfather clock struck 7:15. That meant he'd missed the cocktail hour and they were probably holding dinner for him. Work had kept him late. His parents would understand since they had called the last-minute family dinner meeting just this morning. Austin already had important meetings on the books. He'd gotten away as soon as he could, given the short notice.

As he strode down the hall, he glanced in the living room and could see vestiges of what looked like predinner martinis. Something smelled good. Austin inhaled deeply, and his stomach growled in appreciation. There was nothing like a home-cooked meal. His mom employed a chef who helped her prepare for parties and family gatherings like tonight, but Sarah Fortune could hold her own in the kitchen. She made a mean beef Wellington. Judging by the delicious aroma, that beef Wellington might be on the menu tonight. Austin hoped so as he made his way toward the dining room, where he heard the sound of amicable chatter punctuated by peals of laughter. The sound warmed Austin's heart.

For a moment, he stood in the doorway of the family dining room, taking in the sight of his parents with his four siblings, Beau, Draper, Georgia and Belle. Their brother Nolan and sister Savannah got a pass on tonight's family dinner meeting because they lived in Austin, Texas. They would have to hear secondhand Miles's misgivings about attending the wedding of his half brother Gerald to his long-lost love, Deborah. That was the topic of tonight's summit.

Funny, though, Nolan and Savannah probably regretted missing an opportunity to get together with the family. That's just how they were. They were a close-knit bunch and enjoyed each other's company, respectfully listening when one of them felt it necessary to call a family meeting. To them, family was everything, which made the topic of tonight's meeting so curious. They had all been invited to Gerald and Deborah's wedding in Paseo, Texas. However, based on recent turns of events, Miles believed they should not attend.

"There he is." His mother beamed at him and motioned him inside. "Come in here and give your mama a hug." Even though Austin was thirty-two years old, he did exactly that, following it up with hugs for Belle and Georgia and solid handshakes and backslaps for his father and brothers.

His mother fussed about, offering him a martini. "It's no trouble to mix one up for you right quick." Her Louisiana accent was a bit more pronounced this side of the cocktail hour. Ever the lady, Sarah never overindulged, but she certainly did enjoy a predinner libation.

"Thanks, Mom. I'll have a glass of wine with dinner. I have to drive to airport later."

Soon dinner was served. Just as Austin had hoped, it was beef Wellington, with sides of asparagus with hollandaise sauce, baby carrots and garlic mashed potatoes. It was delicious. Austin hadn't realized how hungry he was. He'd been so busy he'd only had time to eat half the turkey sandwich that Felicity had ordered for him at lunch.

*Felicity.* He made a mental note to talk to his father about creating an advertising position for her. He'd planned to present it as if Felicity had approached him about advancement opportunities within Fortune Investments. He knew his dad well enough to know if he told Miles that she was quitting, he would've thought her unimaginative.

Miles might not realize how hard Felicity worked and how good she was at her job. To Austin, she wasn't just an assistant, she was his right hand. She was the person who kept him on track. She was one of the few people outside of his family that he trusted implicitly. Even though a new position meant she might not be able to do as much for him, he owed it to her. At least she'd still be with Fortune Investments. So, yes, before he left here tonight, he would plant the seed about promoting her.

In the meantime, he would enjoy his meal and this time with his family. During these family meals, food and catching up were first. Business second. They never broached family business until the coffee and dessert course was served.

True to form, after everyone had a generous helping of brandy-laced English trifle, Miles started the discussion.

"I called you here tonight because we've all been invited to Gerald and Deborah's wedding. There's been a lot of discussion about whether or not we should attend."

He sipped his coffee. "As much as I'd love to go, I don't think it's a good idea. With all that's happened lately, gathering the family in one place doesn't seem like a very smart idea. Essentially, it would make us sitting ducks. We'd be an easy target for whoever has been terrorizing the Fortunes."

Miles was talking about a series of events that had taken place over the last five months. It had started with a fire at the Robinson estate in Austin. The fire had injured Gerald's son Ben, though he had recovered. Gerald's company, Robinson Tech, had been targeted, causing the business to have to recall some of their software. The sabotage had even affected the extended family. Fortunato Real Estate, the business of Kenneth Fortunato, Miles's other half brother, had experienced a downturn after being the target of rumormongering. Most recently, events had hit closer to home when Austin's sister Savannah's apartment had been vandalized.

All signs pointed to Gerald's first wife, Charlotte Prendergast Robinson, as the perpetrator. After discovering some unsavory realities about Charlotte's true nature, Gerald divorced her and had gotten back together with Deborah, his first and one true love. They met when Gerald was on the run from his past, but they'd split and lost touch before she'd discovered she was pregnant with his triplet sons.

No one had been able to catch Charlotte in the act. The family was concerned, as she had already proven herself to be a force to be reckoned with. Now that she had been excommunicated from the family, she'd made it clear she had no compunction about wreaking havoc on anyone related to the Fortunes, even if it meant hurting people in the process.

"Maybe not, Daddy," said Belle, her pretty brow furrowed. "This is an important day for Gerald. He's marrying the love of his life. He has more money than he knows what to do with. Since this day is so important to him and Deborah, don't you think he will invest in the best security?"

"I'll bet it will be on par with the Secret Service," said Draper.

"I know," said Belle. "Call me crazy, but I want to go."

Miles looked furious as he sipped his red wine. "She burned down her own house, injuring her own son. A sociopath like that won't rest until she seeks the ultimate revenge."

Miles shook his head. Georgia, who was seated to his left, reached out and took her father's hand. He squeezed hers in return, but the anger was still apparent in his eyes.

"I'm trying hard to embrace my new extended family." Miles used his fingers to make air quotes around the word *family*. "I know you think it's nice to think that we have found this wonderful, big family and that they are welcoming us with open arms. But don't forget, I've lived all but the last six months of my life without them. You—" Miles spread his arms wide and gestured to his wife and grown children gathered around the table and then pounded his fist on his heart "—all of you, and Savannah and Nolan are my family. And you're all the family I need. If anything happened to any of you because of them, I couldn't forgive myself. I say we send Gerald and Deborah a nice gift and our best wishes for a happy life together, but we're staying away."

Miles was still trying to come to terms with the extended family. Not only was he a self-made man, he was also incredibly self-reliant. His birth father, the philandering millionaire Julius Fortune, had denied Miles at birth. Mile's mother, Marjorie Melton, had raised him on her own. When Miles, who had shared his mother's last name, turned twenty-one, Marjorie revealed his father's identity. That's when Miles took on the Fortune surname. He'd done it to prove a point. He didn't want his father's money. In fact, he set his sights on doing well in spite of his heartless father and the Fortunes.

Not only was he driven to achieve financial success, but he wanted a large family to hold close and shower with the love his own father had denied him. It was a subtle way of showing old man Fortune and the myriad others, *I don't need you. You didn't love me, but I'm going to show you how love is done. In the end, you'll be the lonely, broken one on the outside looking in*. It was a silent and dignified middle finger.

Then a strange thing happened; Miles learned that he wasn't Julius's only dirty little secret. There were others. Much like Miles, they, too, had created their own large families and successful lives. Finally, Schuyler Fortunado Mendoza, daughter of Kenneth Fortunado, decided it was time to end all the secrecy and hurt. It was time for all the Fortune family branches to come together. She arranged a family reunion for the "bastard Fortunes," inviting them all to come to the Mendoza Winery in Austin.

Her intentions were pure. She thought she was doing a good thing by bringing everyone together. However, calling the illegitimate Fortunes together actually ended up putting them in danger, which was why Miles and Sarah were having so much trepidation about attending the wedding.

"If we don't go," Belle said, "they might think we're snubbing them. Family relations are a bit tenuous right now since everything is so new. In addition to being there to support Gerald and Deborah, I think this is an important opportunity to claim our rightful place in the Fortune family."

Miles glared at his daughter. "Enough!" he bellowed. "I am the head of this family. I have decided we are not going. End of discussion." His voice was low and simmering as he bit off each word one by one in a way that had everyone holding their collective breath. Once Miles Fortune made up his mind, he didn't tolerate people challenging him like Belle was doing. "If you'll excuse me, I'll say good night."

Scowling, Miles scooted his chair back from the table and left the room. Austin knew now was not the time to broach the subject of creating a new position for Felicity. Miles was not in the mood and it might undermine the promotion. Austin would approach him after he got back from Atlanta.

Felicity had been waiting all day to ask Austin if he'd had a chance to talk to his father about a new position for her. After the talk with Maia, Felicity had a chance to mull it over a bit and the more she thought about it, the more it made sense to stay at Fortune Investments. If she could get promoted within the company she could keep her benefits and they were always so generous with compensation. It would be less like starting over and more like making a strategic career move up the ladder. Plus, she would still be around Austin, just not as close. Maybe if she wasn't always "right there," Austin might feel her absence enough to realize he missed her.

As counterintuitive as that might sound, it made sense. It was like taking the same route to work every day. You got in such a habit that you went about the drive with blinders on, missing the most important sights along the way. One day, you'd notice a house or shop or a tree that you'd driven by hundreds of times and realize it was the first time you'd really seen it.

Felicity propped her elbows on her desk and rested her chin on her fist. She wanted to be Austin's tree. She chuckled to herself. She wanted him to look up and suddenly notice her.

*Notice me, Austin. See me.*

She heard his voice coming from the other side of the corridor. That snapped her out of her daydreaming, and she busied herself on the computer, pretending to type away, adding notes to her to-do list for the Fortune Investments gala. She was way ahead of schedule, but she never wanted to give Austin the impression she was slacking off on the job. If she let down her guard, that would be the time he'd notice her.

Come to think of it, she would be doing herself a favor when she went in to talk to him if she told him she really was enthusiastic about the opportunity to stay on with Fortune Investments. The other day when Austin had mentioned the possibility of creating a position for her, she had been so flustered about giving him her notice that she hadn't even acted very excited about the prospect. She smiled at him as he came closer, cell phone pressed to his ear.

"Mackenzie, seriously?" His laugh was infused with a sexy flirtation that made Felicity's heart drop.

Who was Mackenzie? It certainly didn't sound like a business call. In fact, it didn't sound like any type of call she'd ever heard Austin take out in the open like this. Most of the time his calls were business. The small percentage that weren't were family.

He laughed again.

*Oh, Mackenzie, you funny girl, you.* Felicity stared at her computer screen, so he wouldn't know she was listening.

"Okay. Okay. If you insist. *Macks*, it is." Then he slipped into his office, closing the door behind him.

*Max? Or Macks?*

*As in short for Mackenzie?*

*Either way, it proved they were on personal terms.*

Through the glass wall that divided their workspaces, she watched Austin sit down at his desk and continue the conversation. She couldn't hear what he was saying now, but he was animated. More than she'd ever witnessed before.

His face transformed as he seemed to give a full-throated laugh, his eyes crinkled at the corners, lighting up and dancing. He leaned back casually in his chair, raking his hand through his hair.

She wasn't even bothering to sneak peeks at him now. She was full on staring, greedily watching him delight at whatever it was that this Macks had to say. Of course, Austin was oblivious that she was watching him.

What kind of a woman called herself Macks?

Felicity's phone chirped Maia's text tone. Reluctantly Felicity dragged her gaze off Austin to see what her friend needed.

Are we still on for tonight? Just wanted to make sure you're able to untangle yourself from the Beast.

I'll be there.

ETA?????

6 p.m. as planned

By the time Felicity put her phone in her purse and looked back at Austin, he was off the phone and on his computer.

She needed to borrow a page from this woman and start being more of a *Macks*—not a Mackenzie. Mackenzie sounded prim and proper, like a rule follower. Macks sounded like a woman in charge of her destiny.

Felicity pulled up the interoffice messaging system on her computer and typed, Do you have a moment?

She pressed Send before she could change her mind. It was twenty minutes until five o'clock.

She was going to channel her inner Macks and march in there. First, she was going to tell him she was leaving at five because she had plans. Then she would ask him if he'd talked to his dad. She was not going to sit around and wait for him to come to her. She was going to be proactive.

Austin had been out of the office all day, which meant he would be pulling a late night tonight. Usually, she stayed as late as he did. She didn't mind, as it gave her time to get a jump on future projects such as the FI charity ball. She was single-handedly organizing the ball. It was a big job and took a lot of extra time. But tonight, she had promised Maia she would come to the salon so her friend could practice for the hair show. She said she'd be there at six o'clock. That meant she needed to get a move on if she was going to go home and grab a bite to eat and change out of her work clothes and into something more comfortable before she went to the salon.

She jumped at the sound of the chime notifying her of Austin's reply.

Sure, come on in.

She looked at him, but his head was bent over his desk and he was busy writing something.

Felicity's stomach bunched, then fell as she realized in a matter of minutes, she would know whether or not Miles Fortune was on board for keeping her on board.

The sooner she knew, the better. She gathered her courage and closed the short distance to Austin's office.

"Hey, what's going on?" He leaned back in his chair, laced his fingers together and cradled the back of his head. His biceps pushed at the boundaries of his shirt sleeves. Her gaze lingered. She couldn't help it.

He motioned for her to sit on one of the chairs in front of his desk. She chose the opposite chair from where she'd sat when she'd given her notice.

"What did your father say? I'm dying to know."

His blank stare made her wish she could retract the question.

"What did he say about what?" Austin asked, leaning farther back in his chair, but not looking nearly as relaxed as he had when he was talking to Macks.

"Really, Austin? You don't remember?"

He blinked once. Twice. Then he tapped his head. "Oh, my God, right. I'm sorry. It's been a crazy day."

*I'll bet. Macks must be occupying a lot of real estate up there.*

"I'm sorry, Felicity. I haven't had a chance to bring it up with him. The other night when we were at dinner I intended to talk to him, but it ended up not being a good time. We had some family business to discuss and Belle was pushing his buttons. She got him a little riled up. You know how he can be."

Felicity didn't answer.

It was the stupidest thing but suddenly she felt a hot, stinging sensation behind her eyes. God, she was not going to cry. She couldn't cry. Why did she want to cry over this?

So, he hadn't remembered right off the bat. The guy had a lot on his mind. But suddenly it was crystal clear to her that she really didn't want to leave. She wanted to stay.

Obviously, Austin wasn't so devastated by the thought of her leaving. It was ridiculous, but it hurt her feelings.

Needing to get ahold of herself, she bit her bottom lip hard to keep the tears at bay. It worked.

"No problem," she heard herself saying. Maybe after he'd initially thought up the possibility of creating a position for her, he'd realized it wasn't feasible. Or maybe he had mentioned it to Miles and his father had shut down the idea. Maybe Austin was trying not to hurt her feelings.

"It's five o'clock," she said. "I need to leave. I have plans tonight. I'll call Derek and ask him to bring your dinner to the office. What time do you want him to deliver it?"

"Anytime is fine."

Derek was Austin's personal chef. Usually, Derek left Austin's dinner in the oven of Austin's condo, which was around the corner from the Fortune Investments offices, and Felicity would pick it up and bring it to the office. Tonight, Derek would have to deliver it.

If she was leaving at the end of the month, Austin would need to learn to fend for himself until he got his new assistant up to speed.

It hit her that having someone else deliver Austin's dinner wasn't exactly making him fend for himself, but it was part of the weening process for her. She enjoyed taking care of him. It was a point of pride. Moving on would be a loss for her, too.

She felt his eyes on her. "Are you okay?"

"Sure. Why wouldn't I be?"

"Something's wrong." He shook his head. "I'm sorry I haven't had a chance to talk to Miles. I will as soon as I can. I promise. Okay?"

"It's fine, Austin. Really."

She stood to leave, feeling a little better that he'd noticed that she was upset and had said he would speak to his dad. If Miles had already shot down the idea, Austin wouldn't have said that. She knew him well enough to know that.

"Don't leave me, Felicity. Okay?"

Her mouth went dry at his words.

*Dear God, if you only knew.*

But he didn't. This was strictly business. It would always be about business when it came to them. That was the problem. Her *taking care of* Austin was so personal, sometimes her heart crossed the line. She needed to make sure her mind and better judgment stayed in complete control. Because her heart could only lead her astray.

Still, it didn't help that the look on his face was so earnest it made tears sting the back of her eyes again. God, she was a mess. Her emotions were up and down like a roller coaster. One minute she was ready to walk out the door, and the next minute his *don't leave me* had her wanting to withdraw her resignation and dedicate her life to him... Well, to being his personal assistant. And that was no kind of life. Especially when she felt like this for him.

"Before you leave for the day, would you do me a huge favor? Will you call a courier to deliver this?"

She nodded and reached out, taking the large white envelope he held.

It was addressed to Mackenzie Cole. Felicity recognized the lower Garden District zip code. The name Mackenzie was crossed through on the package. Austin had rewritten *Macks* above it in that script that was so achingly familiar to Felicity. For some stupid reason, seeing Macks's name written by Austin's hand felt so personal. It was a punch to Felicity's gut.

No. She would not call a courier to deliver this package.

Felicity would deliver it herself.

## Chapter Three

Macks Cole was Felicity's worst nightmare.

Felicity knew it had been a mistake to deliver the package herself the moment the tall, willowy Margot Robbie lookalike answered the door. She was exactly the kind of beautiful, worldly woman who would call herself Macks.

Scratch that.

Her old-monied parents had probably called her Macks since birth. She'd probably been named Mackenzie after the great-great grandmother with the money. Her brothers would be Digby and Shep. They probably spent hours on the golf course and drank too much with their Mardi Gras krewe. Of course, there would be a baby sister. Her name would be Margaux, but they'd call her Go, because she was cute and sweet, and they'd already determined Macks was the strong, efficacious girl child.

"May I help you?" Clad in impeccable Eileen Fisher white linen, barefoot with wide stacks of thin gold bangle bracelets on her tanned arms, Macks managed to look both effortlessly sexy and sophisticated.

"Are you Mackenzie Cole?"

She regarded Felicity with the assurance of a woman who was comfortable in her own skin. If Felicity had to guess, she'd peg Macks for midthirties, which meant the woman was probably seven or eight years her senior.

"I am." Her expression was bemused but patient, as if she'd opened the door to find a Girl Scout selling cookies.

*Why did you come here, you idiot? Curiosity killed the cat.*

Or at least it killed the fantasy that she, Felicity, was secretly Austin's type. That there had been a chance for them.

She had been utterly wrong.

"I have a package for you."

She pictured Macks talking on the phone with Austin, alternately reclining on a red velvet chaise longue—she'd pronounce it the French way because she'd know things like that—and sitting in lotus position on the polished cherry mahogany floor in a perfect patch of sunshine. All the while, her white linen would stay as pressed and pristine as the moment she'd removed it from the dry-cleaning bag.

Macks took the envelope and examined the writing. Her eyes flashed, and she smiled a smug, knowing smile. She turned sparkling green eyes on Felicity as if she expected her to deliver a singing telegram that sounded like this:

*Austin says he loves you.*
*Soon you'll be his wife.*
*You're absolutely perfect.*
*You'll have a lovely life.*

"Come in, come in." Macks motioned Felicity inside.

Felicity blinked and balled her hands into fists. For a split second, she wasn't one hundred percent certain she hadn't inadvertently been making jazz hands as she sang the telegram in her head.

Apparently, she hadn't because her arms were rigidly at her sides, and Macks wasn't looking at her like she was a spontaneous performing weirdo.

She should have said no to Macks's invitation to come inside. She was going to be late meeting Maia, but the need to see Macks in her natural habitat overpowered Felicity's preference for punctuality.

Macks closed the leaded stained-glass front door and disappeared down the cherry mahogany hallway. The flooring was the only thing Felicity's imagination had gotten right. The living room, which was to the left, was furnished with expensive-looking pieces that were surprisingly minimalist and modern. Except for the dark wooden floor, the room was done in monochromatic white and punctuated with pops of color from artwork on the wall. Clearly expensive fine art. A freeform sculpture that looked like Chihuly glass was lit in one corner. On the opposite wall was a life-size roughhewn stone sculpture of a man's naked torso showcased from throat to muscular midthigh. It was very lifelike and… um…erect. Felicity felt her cheeks warm.

Now, that was a conversation starter if she'd ever seen one. Did Mr. Erectus have a first name? Was Macks personally acquainted? No? Would she like to be? He looked like a strapping young man. Maybe Macks could date him instead of Austin?

*Just an idea.*

Felicity sighed. She should've called the courier. Because meeting perfect Macks and standing here inside her perfect home was akin to watching a disturbing scene in a movie. She knew she should've closed her eyes, looked the other way. But she didn't. Now she couldn't unsee the reality.

No wonder Austin had been flirting like a schoolboy.

"Here you go." Macks's melodic voice echoed as she approached, one bangle-clad arm outstretched, dangling a twenty dollar bill from her perfectly French-manicured fingers. "This is for you—what did you say your name was?"

*I didn't.*

"I'm Felicity. I'm Austin's assistant. I was in the area on my way to another appointment. I told him I'd drop off the package. So, I can't accept that." She gestured to the money. "Thank you, though."

Felicity flashed her best smile.

Macks was looking at her in a different, more appraising way. "Austin didn't mention that his assistant was so pretty."

Austin had mentioned her?

Maybe in passing. *I'll make sure my assistant puts our first date on the books.*

But he hadn't asked her to reserve a date or make a reservation or—

"Thank you, Felicity." Macks's voice had regained its self-assured, slightly superior tone. She gracefully reached around and opened the front door. Felicity's cue to leave.

"It was *lovely* meeting you," Macks said. "I'm sure this won't be the last time we'll see each other."


"This makeover was a great idea," Felicity said. "I'm glad you roped me into this hair show."

"I didn't intend to rope you into anything," Maia said as she swiped the blending brush over Felicity's face before stepping back and admiring her work like a master artist.

"Roped or not, I probably wouldn't be sitting here tonight if not for the hair show." Felicity stared at herself in the mirror, turning her head this way and that. "Even if it was a ploy, it's okay."

The makeover was subtle. The cut made her hair bouncy. The modest highlights made it shiny. Maia had applied just enough makeup so that Felicity looked polished and put together. This new, more professional look would come in handy when she started interviewing for jobs at the end of the month. Because if Austin had a girlfriend, she did not want to watch it unfold from the front row seat of Fortune Investments.

Even if the money was good, mooning over her boss

and his new girlfriend wasn't. She'd been at Austin's beck and call since she'd started working for him. Her job had dominated her life. She hadn't even dated anyone seriously since college. Sure, she'd told herself that she didn't have time to date. And to what end?

Even if Macks had called her pretty, ultimately, she'd sized Felicity up and decided she wasn't a threat. Of course she wasn't. Austin Fortune dated women like Macks Cole, not Felicity Schafer.

She ran her fingers through her honey blond hair, letting the locks fall through her fingers and cascade onto her shoulders. The highlights were understated. They looked natural, as if her hair had been kissed by the sun.

The FI charity ball was two weeks before her graduation. She would focus on getting through the ball and then put her energy into finding a new job and hiring her replacement.

She nodded as if confirming the plan to herself.

"So, you like?" Maia asked, handing Felicity a mirror and turning her around so she could view the back of her head.

"I love it. I have to admit, I was a little bit skeptical. I didn't know what to expect. I thought you might do something a little more extreme for the show tomorrow."

It was a relief compared to what she'd feared as she'd watched Maia cover her head in foil rectangles that fanned out in all directions, making her feel like some kind of a space-age creature that could transmit radio waves.

Maia smiled at her approvingly. "Didn't I tell you? This show is about everyday, polished looks. There are some shows where they want looks that are pretty out there. But this is you, only better. Right?"

"What? Like Felicity 6.0?"

"More like Felicity 10.0." Maia laughed. "Don't get me wrong. You were perfect exactly the way you were. You're lucky, you can pull off the no-makeup, girl-next-door look, but it doesn't hurt to change things up every once in a while. Who knows, maybe this will make the Beast finally notice you."

Heat flooded Felicity cheeks.

"Maia, shhhh." Felicity pressed her index finger to her lips and looked around to see if anyone in the bustling salon was listening. As if anyone knew who *the Beast* was or would be interested in a twenty-seven-year-old woman's secret crush. Her cheeks warmed again at the ridiculous thought.

Still, she didn't want to talk about him in the busy salon. The last thing she needed was for someone to recognize her as his assistant and put two and two together and report back that she'd been talking about him. Stranger things could happen.

Austin was a prominent New Orleans business figure. More than one magazine had named him one of New Orleans's most eligible bachelors. During the time she'd been his assistant, one woman had befriended her with the ulterior motive of getting closer to Austin. Another woman had been more up-front about her purpose. She'd approached Felicity in a restaurant bathroom and said, "You're Austin Fortune's assistant, aren't you?" It was more than a little creepy since she'd never met the woman. She'd handed Felicity her card. "Will you please have him call me?"

The card had her name, Beverly Sands, and a phone number. Nothing else. "Is this a business matter?" Felicity had asked because she didn't want to take a chance of offending a potential client.

"Oh, no, this isn't about business. I'm a florist. I want to meet him since I'm going to marry him." She'd laughed and for a minute, Felicity thought she was joking and was about to hand back the card. But there was something in the petite brunette's eyes that was a little crazed. *Crazy eyes*, that was the way Felicity had described her to Austin. Big, round blue eyes that didn't blink as she continuously nodded her head while she talked.

They were alone in the restroom. Deciding it was better to be safe than sorry, Felicity said she would relay the message. That afternoon, a big bouquet of flowers arrived for Felicity. The card said, *Thanks for hooking me up. Love, your friend, Bev.*

She'd showed the flowers to Austin. Since they knew Beverly's name and place of employment from the envelope that came with the card attached to the flowers, they were able to find her photo on social media. Austin had supplied the information to security and had insisted on walking Felicity to her car for a solid month. They'd never heard from Bev again, but it had been a good lesson that people may know more than you realize.

Austin was a smart man. Even if a good portion

of New Orleans's female population was in love with him, if word got back to him that someone of Felicity's description was mooning over him in Maia's salon, it wouldn't take long for him to connect the dots back to her.

She'd worked for him all this time without divulging her secret. Why would she want to spill the beans now?

A little voice in the back of her head screamed, *Because when you quit, you're not going to be working for him anymore. You'll be free to make your move. If you don't, Macks will get him. Go for it!*

But that was the thing. She didn't want to be the one to make the move. Was it so wrong to be old-fashioned? To want him to make the first move? Even if he hadn't even given the slightest hint of interest. Even if he didn't see her that way. Plain and simple. She'd humiliate herself if she told him her feelings.

During the time that she'd been his personal assistant, he hadn't been serious about anyone. And she would know because she kept his calendar and scheduled practically every detail of his life, even the occasional first date that never led to a second.

Most wives didn't know their husbands as well as she knew Austin.

She knew that his favorite music was jazz. His childhood pet was a yellow Lab named Bandit. He liked his coffee strong and black. She had it ready for him every morning. He wasn't very talkative in the morning. Even though he got to the office at the crack of dawn, he needed a moment to read the *Times-Picayune* and drink his strong, black coffee, letting the caffeine get into his bloodstream before he was fit to see anyone. His family was the only thing that ever came before work. He had a sweet tooth, which he indulged in moderation, and she blocked off time for him to have daily workouts, which allowed him to enjoy his treats and stay healthy.

Austin Fortune had said it himself. She was his right hand. She anticipated his every mood. She knew him better than he knew himself sometimes, understanding what made him happy and how to preempt the things that didn't. She was his gatekeeper. If anyone wanted to get to him, they had to go through her. Yet, somehow Macks had managed to infiltrate.

Since Austin didn't seem to mind, it was out of her hands.

"There's my best girl." A blond guy walked over and hugged Maia.

"Hey, handsome," she said in her flirty voice.

Who was this? Did Maia have a guy in her life? Why hadn't she mentioned him?

"Thanks for fitting me in on such short notice."

Okay. Maybe he was a client.

Maia prided herself on forming strong bonds with her clients. That's why her business was booming.

But his hair was very short. He didn't look like a haircut emergency. Then again, Felicity was not an expert in this arena. Maybe it was a special cut that needed to be meticulously maintained?

"Yeah, hon, have a seat right there. I've just finished up with Felicity. Have you met Felicity?"

"I haven't had the pleasure. Kevin Clooney." He offered his hand and Felicity pulled hers out from under the cape she'd been wearing while Maia cut her hair. Kevin held her hand a little too long, his eyes sweeping over her face and his mouth widening into a broad smile.

"Felicity Schafer," she said. "I'm Maia's neighbor."

"Maia, babe, you've been holding out on me," said Kevin. "I can't believe you haven't introduced us before now. I'm in love."

*Okay, bring it down a notch or two, bud. People are staring.*

They were. The woman in the station next to Maia's was alternately exchanging glances with Mark, her burly, bald, tattooed hairdresser, and grinning at Felicity and Kevin.

"Felicity is my model for a show tomorrow night," Maia said, as she wet Kevin's hair with water from a spray bottle and combed it through.

Kevin nodded. "You look gorgeous."

Was he flirting with her? "Maia does good work."

"It's easy to do good work when you start with such a good canvas," he said.

"True," said Maia.

As much as Felicity hated it, she felt heat bloom in her cheeks. Doing her best to channel her inner Macks, she pushed her shoulders back, lifted her chin and looked him directly in the eyes. "You're a flirt, aren't you, Kevin?"

Maia snorted. Kevin laughed and so did Felicity.

"He might have been called that once or twice," Maia said.

Kevin held up his hands in a show of surrender. "All I'm saying is that you two are going to own that hair show."

"Yeah, we are," Maia said, her scissors flying as she sheared fractions of an inch off Kevin's hair.

Felicity was just about to say goodbye when Kevin asked, "Is this hair show industry only or is it open to the public?"

"Why?" Maia asked. "Do you want to go? I can get you a ticket if you do."

He slanted a glance at Felicity. "I'd love to. Maybe the three of us could go out for drinks afterward."

"It's a date," said Maia.

*A date, huh?* Felicity had a suspicious feeling she'd just been set up. Maia knew she'd be in the salon. She just happened to fit in Kevin for a haircut he didn't really need.

But Kevin was cute, and he seemed fun. She could give him a chance. She didn't have to marry the guy. If Austin was seeing Macks, maybe having drinks with a cute, fun guy was exactly what she needed.

Austin got to the office at a quarter to seven Monday morning. Felicity was already sitting at her desk working at her computer, as usual. As he walked by and grabbed the cup of coffee she had waiting for him on the corner of her desk, something made him do a double take and stop.

"May I help you?" She kept typing and didn't look away from her computer. She had used her smart-alecky voice. The tone she took when she was about

to point out the obvious after he'd been painfully obtuse about something. The voice that would soften later
and allow them to laugh at whatever it was that needed
correcting.

"Something's different," he said, studying her.

She lifted her brows at him and that's when he realized she was wearing makeup. Or at least more makeup
than she usually wore. Did she wear makeup? Was it
politically correct to tell her he'd noticed?

"You cut your hair." It was a statement. Not a judgment.

"I did." She ran her fingers through the silky-
looking strands.

*Silky-looking.* Now, admitting that might get him
into trouble.

"What do you think?" she asked.

"If I say it looks nice, it won't offend you or make
you feel compromised or objectified, will it?"

Her eyes flashed and there was the briefest second
before she burst out laughing.

"Austin, I asked you what you thought. I'm certainly not going to run and file a harassment charge
with Human Resources."

"Okay, then. I like your haircut. It looks nice. You
look nice."

She smiled and did that fingers-through-the-hair
thing again. This time he noticed that her hair was
shiny and that pieces that caught the light were the
color of honey.

"Thank you, Austin. You, on the other hand, could

use a haircut. You're looking a little untamed there. Do you want me to schedule one for you?"

Now it was his turn to run his fingers through his mop. She was right; it was a little long. "Sure, that would be great. Thanks."

He turned to go, but Felicity said, "Oh, hey, listen. I need to leave at five o'clock again."

She had every right to leave at five. But when he worked late, it was always nice to know she was there, too. Often, it would just be the two of them in the office until late and she'd buzz him and say, "Austin, go home. The work will be here tomorrow."

It's not that he needed her to remind him—well, maybe he did. He liked the office better than home. What was he going to do if she left?

"Do you have something with school going on?" he asked, and added before she could answer, "Be sure to let me know the date of your graduation so I get it on my calendar."

"I've already put it on your calendar. And no, to-night is not about school. I have a date."

*A date? Felicity dates?*

That was another one of those obtuse questions that would send her into smart-aleck mode. Why wouldn't Felicity date? She was beautiful and smart and she had a smokin' hot bod, curves in all the right places. Okay, that was definitely the kind of comment that would send her down the hall to HR faster than he could tell her he hadn't meant anything offensive by it. It was just a fact—like the honey-gold highlights in her hair and the pink stain on her bee-stung lips.

Why was he thinking about this now? And when did Felicity have time to date when she was always working late with him?

"Who's the lucky guy?" he asked, trying not to look at her lips.

"It's a guy named Kevin Clooney. My friend Maia introduced us. We hung out on Saturday."

"Kevin Clooney?" he asked. "Why does that name sound familiar?"

"You're probably thinking George Clooney, the actor. No relation."

No. That wasn't what he was thinking, but—

"You'll get to meet him because he's picking me up at the office."

"Don't you think you should meet him out the first few dates? You don't know this guy. He could be some kind of sociopath."

She squinted at him. "Austin, I thought him picking me up from work was gentlemanly. He's not a sociopath. He's been a client of my neighbor Maia's for years."

"Yeah, but you never know. You can't be too careful these days."

He should've been more careful when his ex-wife Kelly swooped into his life. He'd been duped. Such an easy mark. He didn't want Felicity to rush into anything and find herself in a bad situation.

She was smiling at him now. "Thank you for caring."

He grunted. "Of course."

*I care about you. I'll rip the SOB's head off if he doesn't treat you right.*

Felicity bit her bottom lip, which made him look at her mouth again. Thank God she was studying her computer screen, so she didn't see him looking.

*Kevin Clooney.*

*What a dumb name.*

So that's why she was all dressed up and wearing that pink lip stuff today.

"Hey, listen. Can you stay late tomorrow night and maybe Wednesday, too? We need to talk about the charity ball."

"Sure. That's not a problem."

"Good. Thanks."

Maybe they'd need to work through the weekend, too.

He turned away on a jerky motion that made his coffee slosh and splash onto his crisp white button-down.

He growled and muttered a string of expletives under his breath.

"I heard that, potty mouth," Felicity said. "What did you do?"

"I spilled my damn coffee down the front of my shirt and I don't have a spare in my office. I used the last one Thursday before the McCutcheon meeting."

Cursing again, he frowned down at the stain. He should've put his suit coat on when he got out of his car.

*What a great way to start the day.*

"Now, I have to have to go home and change. I have a meeting at nine and I look like a freaking bum."

"No, you don't," Felicity said. "I'll go pick up your

dry cleaning when they open at eight. You have some white shirts in that order."

"I do?" he said, the edges of his bad mood lifting. "Thanks. So, uh—you're not going to let this guy take you home, are you?"

Felicity's cheeks flushed. "And you were worried that complimenting me on my haircut was inappropriate? That's none of your business, Austin. Who I go home with is kind of private. Don't you think?"

"What? No. That's— No, wait," Austin sputtered. "That's not what I meant. I meant it's not a good idea for you to let a guy you've just met know where you live. Letting him know where you work is bad enough. Take an Uber home. Don't tell him your home address."

Felicity looked a little embarrassed. "Oh. I misunderstood. If it makes you feel any better, he has to drop me off here because my car will be here."

Austin ran a hand over his face. "Yeah, I guess so. Are you in the parking garage?"

She nodded.

"Text me about five minutes before you get here, and I'll come down and meet you."

She scrunched up her nose. "Um, thanks, Dad, but I think I'll be okay. I've been on dates before. This isn't my first rodeo."

He tried to say something, but the words got stuck in his throat and it came out sounding like something between a grunt and a growl. He turned around to go brood in his office.

"Austin, wait a second."

He turned back to her.

"Now you have me second-guessing everything. You're right. I don't know Kevin. I mean, Maia does, but she hasn't dated him. She cuts his hair. I'll call him and tell him I'll meet him at the restaurant. It'll be easier that way."

"Good."

Austin nodded and went into his office. He should've felt better, but he didn't.

What the hell was wrong with him? Why did learning that Felicity had a date throw him into such a tailspin? This was *Felicity*, for God's sake. His assistant. Maybe this date thing and her leaving earlier than usual were underscoring the fact that he really was going to lose her—that Fortune Investments was going to lose her—if he didn't talk to his father soon. He made a mental note to do that today.

He sat down at his desk and stole a glance at her through the glass wall.

Was this the first time he'd been aware of her going out with someone? Until now, it seemed as if he'd never had to share her with another man because he'd always kept her so busy. If he was completely honest with himself, he didn't want to start sharing her now.

God, but not like that. Not in an intimate way. He blinked and shook away the strange feeling lurking in his solar plexus.

What the hell was that all about? Where had it come from? Sure, Felicity was a smart, beautiful woman, but Fortune Investments had a strict no-fraternizing policy. He couldn't allow himself to think about her in any other context than platonic.

He reframed his thoughts.

What he'd meant was he didn't want to share her because he'd grown accustomed to being the sole beneficiary of her efficient capability. She kept him organized and on track. She made him look good. And made it seem so effortless, though he knew damn well it was hard work.

That's why it wasn't fair to her to expect that she would spend the rest of her working life wasting her talent fetching his coffee and picking up his dry cleaning. But what the hell was he going to do without her?

## Chapter Four

The next morning, Felicity sat at her desk, sipping her morning tea, mulling over last night's date with Kevin. He was a good guy, but she wasn't interested in seeing him again.

She was more eager to get back to her desk and resume life as usual.

Early morning was her favorite time in the office. She and Austin occupied the northeast corner of the Fortune Investments building. Since Felicity always arrived at the crack of dawn, it meant the office was still quiet and she could collect her thoughts as she sipped her tea and watched the sun rise over the New Orleans Central Business District.

It put her in a good place, started her day off right. Since Austin had to drink his coffee before he was fit for the world, it sort of felt like they were waking up together. If you didn't count the inconvenience of separate beds, in separate houses.

But even the most serene morning couldn't prepare her for the flowers.

Felicity was on the phone when Carla from the reception desk personally walked the huge arrangement back to Felicity's desk. Carla waited for her to get off the phone before she thrust the stunning bouquet of white lilies, peonies and roses at her, and proclaimed in a singsong voice, "Someone got flowers. Who are they from and most important, what did you do to deserve them?"

"I have no idea," Felicity said. She was surprised that Carla hadn't opened the envelope herself and peeked at the sender. Clearly, Carla wasn't budging until she got the scoop.

Felicity accepted the fragrant bundle and took the card off the holder. With a sinking feeling, she took her time opening the envelope and pulling out the card.

Actually, she had a pretty good idea who'd sent them—and she wished he hadn't. It just felt wrong. All wrong. Then again, they could've come from a vendor she'd been working with for the charity ball. Another perk of being Austin's assistant was that sometimes companies sent incentives and samples, trying to entice her into using their goods and services. There had been a cashmere scarf from the office cleaning service; Belgian chocolates from the paper dealer; a leather day planner embossed with her name from the temp agency they sometimes called on when they needed extra help. In fact, that's how Felicity had found her job at FI. Austin had brought her in as a temp and when she'd had his coffee and newspaper waiting for him without his asking, he'd offered her the job permanently.

So, the flowers could've been from someone else. But no, her first inclination right.

You're still the most gorgeous model in the show. Last night was fun. When can I see you again? Kevin

*No. No. No. No. No.*

But, yeah, Kevin had sent her the flowers. Gorgeous flowers. They must've cost a fortune. If she'd been able to send them back, she would have, because looking at them and reading his candid note produced in her that particular brand of dread that happened when a guy was interested in you but you didn't return his feelings.

She didn't want to hurt his feelings. But she just wasn't into him. Not like *that*. Sure, the date had been…pleasant. He was easy to talk to. He hadn't made her feel bad when she'd turned her head, offering a cheek when he'd leaned in for a good-night kiss.

Yeah… Kevin was a nice guy, she supposed, but he wasn't doing it for her. Something felt off.

She cast a quick glance at Austin, who was concentrating on something on his computer, and her heart hurt for a completely different reason. That caused a host of mixed emotions to flood through her. Why didn't she like Kevin? Why had her heart sentenced her to a lost cause? Sure, Kevin was laying it on kind of thick, but maybe if she let down her guard, maybe if she faced facts, she'd realize it was nice and a lot healthier to open her heart to someone who cared for her. Reflexively, her gaze tracked back to Austin's office. This time he was looking at her.

Her heart leaped into her throat. After it lodged back into place, it thudded in her chest.

"Well? Who are they from?" Carla asked. "Don't leave me hanging."

Felicity shoved the card back in the envelope. "Just a friend."

Out of the corner of her eye she saw Austin stand up from his desk.

"Austin's coming out here. I need to get back to work, and you better get back to the front desk so he doesn't get annoyed with us."

Carla flinched and did a quickstep down the hallway that led to the reception area.

"Don't tell me Bev is back," Austin said.

He looked good today in his charcoal gray suit and white button-down. Of course, he always looked good. Felicity particularly loved that suit on him. It made his shoulders look a mile wide. He was wearing the green paisley tie she liked. It brought out the subtle hazel flecks in his eyes.

Damn him for making her want him when she couldn't have him.

"What are you talking about?"

"Beverly Sands. The flower stalker." Austin gestured to the bouquet.

For some reason the smug look on his handsome face pushed every button she possessed. Everybody knew he could have any woman he wanted—the Macks of the world…the Beverly Sandses…the Felicity Schafers—but did he have to act so self-satisfied?

"These are not from Beverly Sands. Not everything is about you, Austin."

He flinched. Blinked.

*"Gaaaa!"*

Did she really just say that out loud? She'd certainly been thinking it, but she hadn't intended to say it.

A goofy smile spread over his face. "Someone's in a mood."

She bit her bottom lip to keep from pointing out that *he* was usually the one in a mood, but at least *she* had the good grace not to mention it. On those occasions, she tried to lighten the air, not poke the bear.

"These are from Kevin. My date last night."

She held her breath. If Austin made one off-color smirk, one *wink-wink, nudge-nudge, what did you do to merit flowers after a date*, she was going to quit on the spot. Let him book his own restaurant for the first date with Macks.

The silly grin that had previously been on Austin's handsome face darkened. "Kevin Clooney?" He spat out the words like they tasted foul.

"Of course. Who else?"

"Looks like Kevin Clooney wants another date." Felicity shrugged.

"Tell me you're not going out with him again—uh, never mind. I shouldn't have said that. Who you date is none of my business. I hope he treats you like you deserve to be treated. Don't settle for anything less."

Profound words coming from the man who didn't even realize she was a woman.

Scowling, Austin said, "I need to make a call." He turned around and walked away, mumbling something that sounded like, "You could do better than Kevin Clooney," leaving Felicity more confused than ever.

He stepped inside his office, then he leaned out of the doorway and said, "We're still on for tonight, right?"

"Yes, of course."

He gave her a curt nod and ducked back inside.

*You could do better than Kevin Clooney.*

If she was a complete idiot, she might let herself believe his sudden mood change meant he cared. But, of course, he cared. It was more than that. This went deeper. She was picking up a vibe that suggested his mood stemmed from…jealousy?

White-hot currents of electricity coursed through her. She glanced at Austin, but he was on the phone, scowling up at the ceiling, looking impatient.

How had a beautiful bouquet of flowers sent everyone's morning south?

She knew she'd be setting herself up for a world of hurt if she tried to read anything into this other than what it was: Austin was afraid that if she started dating, she wouldn't be as available as usual for the remainder of time she was there.

What was wrong with her? Why was she being such a masochist? Kevin was making all the right gestures. He wasn't playing the "wait three days to call" game, which was refreshingly candid.

Felicity sighed. Maybe she should follow Kevin's

example? Platonically, she could tease and throw innocent barbs at Austin. She could pull him back into line when he needed a reality check, but when it came to matters of the heart, she couldn't tell him how she really felt about him.

Her own reality check was she probably never would tell him how she felt—especially now that Macks was in the picture.

Maybe she should give Kevin a chance. It didn't mean she had to marry him, and at least she'd be investing in someone who treated her the way she should be treated.

Austin stared at the bottom line on the statement he'd been analyzing for the better part of an hour, and realized he had no idea what he'd just read.

He hadn't been able to focus on work since his exchange with Felicity this morning. What the hell was wrong with him? Work was always his escape. When the outside world felt like it was closing in, he'd bury himself in work, which was easy to do at Fortune Investments.

Usually.

Until now.

Felicity was free to see whomever she wanted. Even if it was this Kevin Clooney.

Austin scrubbed his hand over his eyes. He knew it was unfair to form a judgment like this without even meeting the guy, but something didn't feel right. That name was familiar—and not in a good way. But he couldn't place the guy. After discovering how his ex-wife, Kelly, had played him for a fool when she'd set her sights on marrying a Fortune, he'd become exceedingly good at sizing up people and situations. Sometimes only based on a feeling.

Why the hell was Clooney sending Felicity such elaborate flowers after just one date? Austin had been plagued by the question since he'd seen the flowers and Felicity had gotten a little snippy over his questions about Kevin.

What was even crazier and harder to come to terms with was his dread over the reality that he was losing Felicity. In more ways than one. She wanted to move on and leave him behind, and the damnedest thing was it felt more like a breakup than simply losing his assistant. He knew that was unfair and ridiculous and not right on so many levels. She had every right to move on, to find a better situation for herself. He understood.

Part of the problem that he'd realized with the delivery of those damn flowers was that if she left, he might not see her again. For nearly five years, she was usually the first person he saw in the morning and often the last face he saw in the evening. And since it wasn't unusual for him to phone her about business after hours, she was often the last voice he heard before retiring for the night.

He watched her as she wrote something on a legal pad. Probably notes about the ball that she wanted to discuss at their dinner meeting tonight. Or maybe she was mapping out her résumé.

The light coming in from the windows picked out the honey highlights in her hair. She was wearing a black tank and a black pencil skirt that hugged her curves. He'd noticed that this morning. She was wearing that pink lipstick again and she'd styled her hair in the new way she'd been wearing it.

He raked his hands through his hair, fisting them at the nape of his neck.

He needed to give her a reason to stay, even if she would be working in a different department and he'd have to hire a new assistant. That's the only thing that quelled the near panic he felt at the thought of never seeing her again.

The first order of business would be to get his father excited about creating an advertising position for her. He'd left a message for his dad yesterday, asking if they could meet to talk about something important. When Miles's assistant called back, she had informed Austin that his father was out of town this week. She offered to schedule a phone meeting, but knowing Miles the way he did, this was a conversation best done in person.

Felicity just needed to hang on a bit longer. He'd tell her as much at dinner tonight.

In the meantime, it would do him good to be a little less gruff toward her. He knew he wasn't always the easiest person to deal with. Nobody liked working with a bear. But she had always been so good about pulling him out of his dark moods.

It suddenly dawned on him how badly he'd taken her for granted.

It would behoove him to slow his roll and soften his approach.

"How was your day?" Austin stopped when he reached Felicity. He leaned a hip against the corner of her desk and looked at her expectantly. Like he was interested.

*This is weird.*

When was the last time he'd asked her about her day? Um, never. For that matter, when was the last time he stopped to talk about something personal? Well, other than to harangue her about Kevin. And the flowers.

When they talked, they talked about him. Or about work. He usually didn't get into her business. Not that she minded.

She could see the bouquet in her peripheral vision. Austin was on her left side. The flowers sat on the right side of her desk, as if standing in proxy for Kevin.

"It's going well," she said cautiously, her hands poised on her computer keyboard, her heart thumping in her chest.

*Please don't hassle me about Kevin and ruin it.*

"Good." He nodded enthusiastically. "Good."

There was an awkward pause as she waited for him to get to the point.

Oh! Maybe he'd talked to Miles. He would've called her into his office if it was bad news or maybe he would've waited to broach it tonight at dinner. He was smiling at her. Maybe this was his way of delivering good news.

She pushed in her computer keyboard drawer and put her hands in her lap. "Did you talk to your dad?"

Austin's smile faltered. "No. But I did call him yesterday to set up a meeting. He's out of town. I figured it would be best if I talked to him about this in person. Peggy is not sure how long he'll be gone. It could be a week. It could be less. I'll get something on the books as soon as he gets back. I've been meaning to ask you... how is school going?"

Felicity blinked at the non sequitur.

"Fine. I'm all set for graduation. All I have to do is pass the finals."

He was nodding again, maintaining eye contact.

*Those eyes.* She could get lost in those eyes and happily never find her way back to reality.

"Felicity?"

Oh, God, had he asked her a question?

"I'm sorry, what?"

"I asked if your family was coming in for your graduation?"

"Well, my mom lives in New Orleans. So, she'll be there."

"I didn't realize your mom was local. What about your dad?"

*Ugh.* She should've seen that question coming. She should've headed it off before he'd had a chance to ask. She didn't like to talk about her dad.

"No, just my mom. And Maia. You know, my friend who owns the salon." She flipped her hair with her right hand and felt dumb for doing that. "She's the one who did this." She raked her hand through her hair and let it fall back into place. "For that hair show last week."

Those eyes were still on her. She didn't want to love it, because that's how she got hurt. But dammit, she did.

"Have you ever been to the restaurant R'evolution?"

"Is that the one over on Bienville Street?"

"That's the one. I made reservations for us."

*Shut the front door. What?*

First, he'd made a reservation for their dinner rather than just showing up somewhere and working his magic in person—or having *her* make the reservation. All she had to do was call any restaurant in town and say Austin Fortune would like a table. It didn't matter how far in advance the average person had to reserve a table, they would make room for Austin at a moment's notice, because he was Austin Fortune.

The fact that he'd made the reservation himself... Okay, she was not going to read anything more into that than...

*Than what?*

R'evolution was in the French Quarter, across Canal Street and down some ways from the Roosevelt Hotel. While it was in the general area of the hotel where they were having the ball, it was still a surprise. They could have easily just grabbed tapas in the hotel's Fountain Lounge. Or if Austin wanted to be fancy, they could've popped into Domenica, the Roosevelt's Italian restaurant.

She certainly wasn't complaining. She was too off-kilter for that.

"Is R'evolution okay?" he asked. "We can go somewhere else if you like."

"It's fabulous. I've always wanted to try it."

"It's a date, then."

Felicity bit the insides of her cheeks. Clearly, he had no idea what he just said. It wasn't a date. It was a business meeting...for which he'd made a reservation for two at a fabulous restaurant. But she wasn't going to point that out and embarrass him.

"I have a meeting," he was saying, "but I should be ready to go by 6:30. I thought we could leave the office and go to the Roosevelt and check out the space first. We should have plenty of time to make our 7:45 reservation."

"Oh, you were going to come back to the office?" she asked. "I'm looking after Maia's dogs while she's out of town this week. I need to go home and let them out. Should I meet you at the Roosevelt?"

"There's no sense trying to park two cars downtown," he said. "I'll swing by and pick you up at 6:30. Does that give you enough time to take care of the animals?"

She paused, waiting for him to say, *Just kidding*. But it wasn't like Austin to joke like that.

"Sure. 6:30, it is. I'll text you my address."

As he walked down the hall, Felicity watched him, feeling like she'd just entered the twilight zone.

Fifteen minutes later, she was jotting down questions for the rep at the Roosevelt and pondering the new dilemma—should she change clothes or wear the skirt and blouse she'd worn to work?—when her desk phone buzzed. It was Carla at the front desk.

"Hey, 'Liss, there's someone here for Austin. Her name is Macks Cole. She says she doesn't have an appointment, but she'd like to talk to him."

Felicity could hear her pulse in her ears. Macks was here? Her antenna had probably pricked up, warning her that another female was encroaching on her man.

"Tell her to have a seat. I'll be right there."

So, this time Macks had come to Felicity's door. Or actually, Austin's door was probably more accurate.

Felicity checked her posture and took a deep breath before she turned the corner into the reception area.

"Ms. Cole, hello. How may I help you?"

Macks pinned her with the same bemused expression she'd worn the other day when Felicity had shown up at her door. As if Felicity had greeted her speaking some sort of goo-goo-ga-ga baby-talk gibberish. Today she was wearing an all-black ensemble: skinny jeans, a fitted shell and an oversize, long-sleeve maxi cardigan that fell all the way to her ankles and looked butter-soft. Her feet were clad in patent leather platform sandals. Her makeup was minimal, except for black winged eyeliner and shiny, candy-apple red lip gloss coloring her perfect cupid's bow mouth.

She looked as if she'd just stepped off the runway of a Calvin Klein show at fashion week.

"Hello again, Felicity. I'm here to see Austin, please."

As if his sole purpose was to sit around the office, waiting for her to grace him with her presence.

"I'm sorry, he's in a meeting." Felicity eyed the white envelope in Macks's hands. "May I give him a message for you?"

Macks frowned. Her gaze darted around the reception area as if she didn't believe Felicity and expected to see him hiding behind a plant along the far wall.

"Will he be long? I'll wait."

"I'm afraid he'll be tied up for the rest of the afternoon. Is that for him?"

Felicity nodded at the envelope Macks was holding with both hands, as if reluctant to give it up.

"It is. It's an invitation to the opening of an art exhibition at my gallery."

*Oh, so she owns a gallery. Okay. That explains the art in her apartment—and Mr. Erectus.*

Felicity reached out to take the envelope. Macks didn't give it up.

With her outstretched hand, Felicity gestured to the invite. "I'll see that he gets it."

For a moment Felicity feared that Macks might decide to take the invitation with her and attempt delivery another time. Finally, she relinquished it.

"Thank you, Felicity." Macks's red lips tilted up in a tight-lipped smile. "Tell Austin I'm sorry I missed him."

As she watched the woman walk away, she couldn't help but wonder if Austin had taken it upon himself to book dinner reservations for himself and Macks, the same way he'd booked their dinner at R'evolution. She would never know. She'd better get used it, because once she left Fortune Investments, he'd likely be out of her life forever.

## Chapter Five

Austin arrived at Felicity's house a few minutes earlier than he'd promised. He parked on the street and took a minute to take in the neat green double shotgun-style home with its symmetrical front porch decorated with darker green gingerbread embellishments, potted topiaries and hanging ferns.

Before tonight, he'd never really pictured where Felicity lived, but if he had, this would be the place. It was perfectly her. He let himself out of his red Tesla and in through the gate of the waist-high wrought iron fence that surrounded the tidy little front yard, then made his way up the brick path toward her front door. Hers was the left half, with the corresponding address in brass numbers above the threshold.

He glanced at his watch before knocking on the

door. He was a full ten minutes early. But her car was in the driveway and surely it couldn't take very long to do what she needed to do for Maia's dogs. If she wasn't ready to go, he could wait.

Tonight, patience and kindness were the key words.

"You're early," she said when she answered the door. Austin noticed she'd traded in her sleek black pencil skirt and pumps for a blue dress and strappy sandals.

"Sorry," he said, glancing around, taking in the nicely furnished living room. Its hardwood floors and brightly colored furniture added a feminine touch to the otherwise traditional room. It was on the tip of his tongue to tell her how nice she looked, but he reeled the words back in the nick of time. "We have time. Go ahead and finish whatever you were doing."

Although, he couldn't imagine that she needed to do anything else to herself because she looked gorgeous.

"No problem, but here." She handed him a pretty gold necklace. "Will you help me with this? It's difficult to put on by myself."

"Sure." As he put the necklace around the front of her, she held her hair up, allowing him a better look at the fine clasp on the piece of jewelry. He could also see the delicate curve of her neck, which was just long enough to be graceful, and the gentle sweep of her jaw-line. He leaned closer, trying with clumsy fingers to hook the necklace into place—it really would be difficult to manage alone. Not that he thought Felicity had ulterior motives.

Okay, maybe it had crossed his mind.

But then he got a whiff of her perfume, a delicate floral scent. It not only made him want to lean in closer and nuzzle her neck, claim that recess where neck flowed into collarbone, but for a split second, his mind blanked on all the reasons he shouldn't do it and his most primal urges took over.

Thank God he checked himself just in time.

What the hell was going on with him? What were these feelings? And what the hell was he supposed to do with them? As Felicity's boss, he could hardly put the moves on her to test them out.

He finally hooked the blasted necklace together and took a safe step back.

"Thanks." She let her hair loose and it cascaded down around her shoulders. His groin tightened, and he shifted his weight from one foot to another hoping to lessen the tension. "I just need to bring the dogs in. They're out in the backyard taking care of business. Do you want a drink? I have wine and beer in the fridge."

"Thanks, but I'm fine," he said as he followed her out the back door and down three steps to a bricked patio. The plants and flowers were lush and made him think of the book *The Secret Garden*, which his mom had read aloud to him and his siblings when they were younger. "Did you plant all this?"

Felicity beamed and stood up a little straighter, as if it were a point of pride. "I sure did. I love plants and flowers. Gardening is my therapy."

At the sound of her voice, three corgis bounded onto the patio from the yard. With their tongues lolling out the side of their mouths and the playful way they barked and bounced around each other, they reminded

Austin of a trio of tumbling court jesters. Exactly what he needed to lighted the mood.

"Someday, I'd love to put a greenhouse right over there." She pointed to a small section of yard past the patio. "That would be my idea of heaven." She bit her bottom lip. "And that probably makes me seem like I lead a very dull life."

"No, it doesn't," he said. "It makes you seem like you know what you like, like you're very connected to your home and the earth around it."

Her lips curved into a slight smile and her cheeks colored. Felicity of the sharp wit and no-nonsense demeanor suddenly looked vulnerable. He realized that she was very good at taking care of others—at taking care of him—but she wasn't used to being the focus.

"And that's a compliment, in case you were wondering," he added.

"Thank you. Taken as such."

This first glimpse inside her world only made him curious to know more.

Austin had been a good sport listening to her talk about her garden dreams. She felt a little foolish going on about it. The Fortunes had a staff of workers who tended the gardens of their beautiful Garden District mansion. A woman who liked to get her hands dirty was probably about as unattractive to Austin as it got. But he had been a good sport about it, complimentary and indulgent, actually.

At least she always made sure her fingernails were scrubbed clean. Maybe that was why he was so surprised to learn gardening was her hobby. Macks of the immaculate French manicure probably would think such an interest quite plebeian. Oh, well, it was her loss.

One thing Felicity never had trouble with was being herself. Even after being on the outside looking in to the glamorous world of Austin Fortune, she had never forgotten her place. Tonight, as she and Austin had walked the gorgeous, gilded ballroom of the Roosevelt Hotel checking and double-checking the details for the ball, she had never been more aware of her role as facilitator. She would attend the party, but she would be working. She would not be there to have fun or donate money to the cause or have any opportunity to forget exactly who she was and where she came from.

After the walkthrough, she reminded herself of that as she and Austin sat at a lovely table for two in a cozy corner of R'evolution.

It was a banquette-style table, a built-in semicircle covered in soft, tufted white leather, just big enough to make a cozy space for two people. The good part about the bench seating was it forced them to sit next to each other, which meant eye contact was optional and she might not completely give away her feelings for him. The bad part was it forced them to sit next to each other, which meant she could smell his cologne, an intoxicating scent that smelled expensive, with hints of cedar, coffee and leather.

She'd caught whiffs of his scent before as he passed by her desk or leaned in to hand her paperwork to process. But tonight, Austin sat with his body angled toward hers, first, talking business—about the final details they needed to firm up for the charity event, then venturing into the personal realm—asking her questions about herself, her past, her future.

Felicity was not used to having so much of his attention focused on her, which was a little uncomfortable. He was talking to her, learning about her like she'd hope a guy would if they were out on a date.

*This is not a date.*

After the server took their order, Felicity turned the tables on Austin, asking him questions that she would ask a date. Though she knew most of the answers, tonight he seemed different, an open book, his mood lighter, and she fully intended to mine him for what she could get. She was pleasantly surprised by how he opened right up and answered candidly.

"My sister Savannah—have you met her?"

"I did at one of the company picnics. She's the one who's going to school in Texas, right?"

"Yes, in Austin. She and her boyfriend are in town. I'm eager to see her. They're staying with my parents and they'll be here for the ball."

"It will be nice to see her again," Felicity said.

Felicity started to ask Austin if she should seat Savannah and her beau at his table or at their parents' table, but she stopped herself. If she turned the conversation back to work, it might break this delicate spell that seemed to be cast over the evening. Instead, she made a mental note to talk about seating charts when they were back in the office, which would happen soon enough. Too soon for her liking, in fact.

*Why can't this night last forever?*

That way, she wouldn't have to remind him about Macks's invitation, which she'd left on his desk to make sure that he saw it and didn't somehow push it aside.

As if he read her mind, he said, "Did Mackenzie Cole stop by this afternoon?"

A curse word that wasn't usually part of Felicity's vocabulary popped in her brain. They really were on the same wavelength tonight. But why did he have to pick up on her thoughts of Macks? Then again, maybe it was better that it was the Macks train of thought rather than the other, more private tidbits she'd been pondering.

Plus, this provided the perfect opportunity to do a little digging.

*And he called her Mackenzie. Not Macks. Hmm... is that good or bad? Or does he only call her Macks in private? When it's just the two of them.*

"Yes, she came by with an invitation for an art show opening. I put it on your desk."

"I saw it."

"Are you going? I mean, should I put it on your calendar?"

Her heart thudded in her chest as she waited for the moment of truth.

He shrugged, as if he hadn't even considered it. "It's a show at her gallery. I've never heard of the artist. So, I don't know if I'll go."

Inwardly, she cheered.

*Felicity one. Macks zero.*

"Yeah, maybe I will. It would be nice to support her."

*Why does she need your support? She's the kind of woman who gets everything.*

*Felicity zero. Macks one million.*

"She's pretty." Felicity figured she might as well go for broke and get to the heart of the matter.

"Is she?"

"Hello? Have you not met her? She's gorgeous."

*Calm down. You're not trying to sell Austin on her.*

"I have, but—"

"She seems like your type."

*Is she your type, Austin?*

Stepping this close to the edge and looking down on the truth gave her a strange sense of vertigo that made her feel vaguely dizzy and queasy.

The observation seemed to catch him off guard.

"My type? I'm not sure I have a type."

"I mean she's pretty and seems sophisticated and..."

He shrugged. "Yeah, well, even if she was my type, as you say, she's a prospective client. It might get weird."

Momentarily bolstered by Austin's seeming lack of interest in Macks, Felicity let herself daydream a moment, pretending that the people who were dining around them looked at Austin and her, sitting cozy in the corner and deep in conversation, and thought they were on a date. Or that they were a couple.

She tried to shut out the dissident voice in the back of her mind, warning herself not to get her hopes up, because it would be a long, hard fall if she was mistaken.

"Finally! It's about time I get to see my big brother." Standing just inside the foyer, where the elevator opened into Austin's Central Business District pent-house condo, Savannah Fortune threw her arms around Austin. "You'd better have a good reason for not being at Mom and Dad's last night and it better have to do with a woman."

"Yeah, well, not everyone is as lucky as you two lovebirds." Austin turned to Savannah's boyfriend, Chaz Mendoza, and offered a handshake.

"Chaz, good to see you, man."

Chaz gripped Austin's hand and clapped him on the back. Then he moved back to Savannah's side, putting an arm around her waist. The two of them appeared so happily in love they were virtually glowing.

Austin ushered them inside, went to the kitchen and brought back three IPAs.

"Does anyone want a beer stein? I have some in the freezer."

"No, I'm good," the couple said in unison. They sat on the couch so close to each other, legs touching, pos-sessive hands on each other's thighs, that they almost seemed to have morphed into one being.

Austin was glad to see his sister so happy.

As the trio sipped their beers, they chatted about life, catching up on the small things that mattered: how school was going for Savannah; what was new at the Mendoza Winery, where Chaz worked as their secu-rity specialist in addition to doing independent security work; the latest happenings at Fortune Investments; and what was happening in the search for the person or people that had been terrorizing the extended For-tune family.

"I'm glad you're living with Chaz." Austin held up a hand to stop his sister from going on a tirade about how she was perfectly capable of taking care of herself. "Not that you can't handle yourself, but I can't help but worry about you after what happened."

Savannah shrugged. Much to Austin's surprise, she looked resigned to not putting up a fight. It was amazing how she'd mellowed after the break-in and her subsequent move-in with Chaz.

"I feel safer living with him," she said. "That way, I don't have to worry about either of us. After all, the Mendozas have been longtime friends of the Fortunes and several members of the Mendoza family have married Fortunes. Who says their family won't be next? But anyway, all signs still point to Charlotte Prendergast Robinson being the culprit." Savannah shook her head. "Have you heard the latest developments in the search for her?"

"No, what's going on?" Austin sipped his beer and leaned forward, eager to hear the update.

"From what we've heard—and this is from a reliable source—Kate Fortune is calling in all her favors and has used her influence to track down Charlotte. Kate is being merciless." As the matriarch of the Fortune family, Kate Fortune had a vested interest in protecting her relatives and she had the resources to do it. "Everyone is expecting Charlotte to be brought in for questioning any day now."

"Any day now?" Austin asked. "That means she's still out there. Why hasn't she been found yet?"

"It's not that easy," Chaz said. "She's pretty slippery.

From what I hear she knows we're on to her, which sent her deeper into hiding."

"Good," Austin said. "Maybe she'll stay in her cave and leave us the hell alone."

"We hope so, too," Chaz said. "Unfortunately, she seems to pride herself on catching us off guard. She lulls us into a state of complacency and then she strikes again. Savannah and I are not getting complacent. Not after what she did to Savannah's apartment. We're lucky Savannah wasn't there when she broke in. If she had been, who knows how it would've turned out."

"You're not considering going back to your apartment, are you?"

"Nope. Not unless he kicks me out." She smiled up at Chaz, who pulled her in closer.

"Not if I have anything to say about it," he said. "Not even after that woman is behind bars where she belongs."

They played kissy face for a minute, cooing at each other and giving pecks on the lips.

"God, you two. Get a room, will you?"

Inexplicably, Austin's mind flashed back to last night with Felicity. He had as easy a rapport with her as Savannah had with Chaz. Only things seemed so much less complicated for his sister and her boyfriend. Why did the situation have to be so damn difficult with Felicity? If not, last night when he'd walked her to up to the door, he would've leaned in and sampled those lips to see if they were as delicious as they looked. But he'd managed to shove his hands in his pockets and keep a respectable amount of space between them. All in the name of propriety. And not making her uncomfortable.

And, of course, because he was her boss, there was the issue of sexual harassment. But would it be so if they were both willing participants? The trickiest part about it was not to assume he knew how she felt about it. To not let himself get so carried away with the moment that he totally read all her signals wrong. Of course, the easiest way would just be to ask. But "do you mind if I kiss you?" would be just about the most unromantic way that he could think of to profess his feelings.

And what were his feelings? Other than suddenly being overcome with the knowledge that he didn't want her out of his life, he didn't know what else he was feeling.

That was why it wouldn't be fair to Felicity to open that Pandora's box.

And, of course, that meant no kissing her just to see what it was like.

"So, where were you last night?" Savannah asked. "You never answered my question."

"You never asked," Austin said.

"I did so. I said, 'You'd better have a good reason for not being at Mom and Dad's last night and it better have to do with a woman.'"

For a fleeting second, Austin thought about saying he'd been with Felicity, but Savannah knew Felicity and since Felicity was a beautiful woman, his sister would take that and run all kinds of ways with it.

"I had a business dinner."

"Well, that sounds boring."

Austin shrugged as he took a sip of his beer.

*Actually, it was one of the more enjoyable business meetings I've had in a while. One of the more enjoyable evenings, in fact.*

Thrown off the scent, Savannah changed the subject. "This is such a great condo, Austin. Who decorated it for you? Surely, you didn't do it yourself."

"No, I hired that designer Mom uses every once in a while."

For the most part, their mother, Sarah, decorated the family home herself. She had great taste, a generous budget and the time to shop for just the right pieces to achieve the desired look. If she couldn't find it herself, that's when she called in a professional.

"It hardly looks lived in. Does that mean you're spending most of your time at the office?"

He glanced around at the stark beige and chrome furniture and fixtures. He'd been meaning to frame some family photos to add a more personal touch to the space, but he hadn't gotten around to it. He'd bought the place because of the proximity to work and the million-dollar view of Lafayette Square. Given the fact that he really did only sleep there, it wasn't surprising that it didn't look lived in. Austin shrugged. "Duty calls."

"All work and no play will make Austin a very dull boy," Savannah said. "You know you're not getting any younger. When are you going to settle down?"

"Gee, thanks for the reminder, sis."

On one hand, she was right. At thirty-two, he wasn't getting any younger. However, he was in the prime of his business life. Besides, he'd already tried married life and it hadn't worked out.

"Been there, done that, not going back again," he said. "I learned the hard way that I'm just not cut out for marriage."

"Do I need to stage an intervention? Or a round of speed dating to get you out there in the dating world? I really think you just haven't met the right woman yet."

"Even if I did meet *the one*," Austin said, "it wouldn't be fair to get involved with someone who was looking for something as serious as marriage, because I'm married to Fortune Investments."

*Which is why Felicity and I work so well. She understands my career. She's like my work wife.*

As if the grace of God had staged an intervention, Austin's door buzzer sounded, indicating someone was downstairs. He had no idea who it was, but he was grateful to them for providing an interruption.

He excused himself and went to the intercom on the wall by the elevator. "Yes?"

"Hey, Austin, it's Felicity. I'm so sorry to bother you. I know you're spending time with your sister, but I have some papers that need your signature. They're time sensitive and need to be in today. Do you want me to come up or will you come down and sign them?"

Felicity hated to intrude. Austin and his sister were close, and Felicity knew he didn't get to see her as often as he liked. That's why when she visited, he took a rare day off. The last thing he needed was for Felicity to barge in, distracting him with work-related issues. She wouldn't have bothered him if this hadn't been time sensitive.

In the elevator on the way to the top floor of Austin's building, Felicity took a deep breath and checked her posture. She was glad she'd worn a simple, black, sleeveless dress and black slide sandals. She anchored the file folder with the papers under her arm and smoothed the skirt with her palms. It was a comfortable outfit but still looked pulled together enough to feel good about this impromptu visit and seeing Austin's sister again.

It wasn't the first time she had been in his condo. In fact, she stopped by several times a week, on the evenings when Austin worked through dinner, to pick up the meals Derek, his personal chef, prepared for him and left in the kitchen's warming drawer. But it was the first time she had been in the condo with him at home.

The elevator doors opened, and Felicity gripped the folder with both hands and stepped into the foyer.

"We're in the living room," Austin called. "Come on in."

Austin, Savannah and a good-looking guy she hadn't yet met all looked up expectantly as she entered the room. They were all holding beer bottles and looking quite content.

Austin stood.

"Felicity!" Savannah handed her beer to the guy she was sitting next to and jumped up to greet her with a warm hug that made her feel as if she was her long-lost best friend. "I'm so glad I got to see you on this trip. It's been too long. Chaz, this is Felicity Schafer. Austin would be lost without her. Seriously, he wouldn't know his next move without her. Felicity, this is my boyfriend, Chaz Mendoza."

After she and Chaz exchanged pleasantries, Savannah took Felicity by the hand and led her over to the space on the couch next to Austin. "Sit down and join us. Can I get you a beer?"

"Thank you, but I'm just here for Austin to sign papers. I wouldn't have bothered him with it, but I have to scan them and send them off before the end of the day."

Felicity glanced at Austin to gage his reaction. She wanted to stay—even if it was only for a minute, but she didn't want to intrude.

"Join us," he said. "Please."

His invitation spawned a crop of goose bumps on her arms. She ran her hands, envelope and all, over them.

"Savannah, get her a beer," he said. "You do like beer, don't you?"

Savannah and Chaz disappeared into the kitchen before she could decline.

"Is that okay?" she asked. "I don't want to be rude to your sister by refusing, but I hate to intrude on your time together." She held her breath. In a way, it felt as if she was testing the vibes she'd felt last night at dinner, but everything felt a little off-kilter.

"Sit down," Austin said. "It's fine."

Discreetly, she inhaled a deep breath. Right now, a beer and some time with Austin sounded exactly like what she was craving.

She lowered herself onto the edge of the couch. Austin was sitting on the middle cushion. She sat next to him, leaving a respectable amount of space between them.

"Do you want to sign these now?" She held out the file. "It would be just like me to have a beer and go off without you signing them."

He smiled at her in that way that made her wonder what he was thinking. "Then you'd have to come back and have another beer and you probably wouldn't make it back to the office." He smiled, and her heart melted a little more.

"Great, thanks for reminding me," she said. "If anyone at the office smells beer on my breath, I'll need you to tell them it was okay."

"If anyone questions you, just send them to me."

"Even your dad?"

"He's out of town, remember?" Austin said with a grin.

Felicity's stomach knotted, but that's when Savannah and Chaz came back into the room. As Savannah stood in front of her offering her the beer, she looked back and forth between Felicity and Austin with a knowing expression on her face.

"Thank you," Felicity said. She accepted the beverage that Savannah had poured into a frosty mug.

"Maybe it would be a good idea for me to sign the papers now," Austin said, seemingly oblivious to his sister's smile. He took the file and used the pen Felicity had clipped to the front of the folder, wanting to be prepared in case he had wanted to meet her down in the lobby to sign. "Do you have the email address where they need to go?"

"Yes, it's on a sticky note on the inside of the cover."

Austin checked and tapped it with his finger. "Be right back."

"Are you sure you don't want me to do that for you?" Felicity asked. She knew there was a scanner in his home office. It was the same model they used in the FI office. "I'd be happy to."

Austin waved away her offer. "I've got this. Relax and enjoy your beer."

After Austin was out of the room, Savannah asked, "How long have you been with Fortune Investments now, Felicity?"

"It's been almost five years."

"Has it really been that long? I remember when you started. Seems like yesterday."

"Seems that way to me, too."

"Does that brother of mine treat you all right?"

"Austin's a great boss," Felicity said. "How many bosses take their assistants to dinner at a place like R'evolution? Are you familiar with that restaurant?"

Savannah's eyes widened as she nodded. "Of course. It's a great place. Very romantic."

*Yes, it was. Very.*

But she didn't admit that to Savannah. "Well, I don't know about that."

"When were you there?"

"Last night."

Savannah's eyes lit up and Felicity got the feeling that she'd just revealed something she shouldn't have. Suddenly, she felt like she was swimming in water way beyond her depth.

"When were you where?" Austin asked, returning to the living room.

Felicity turned and saw him standing behind her holding the folder of documents he'd scanned and emailed. Her cheeks warmed. She hadn't heard him enter the room. How much of the conversation had he overheard and what did he think of her talking to Savannah about their dinner last night?

That Savannah was a wily one. She seemed to have a talent for getting people to talk about things they shouldn't. Felicity didn't believe Savannah was doing this out of malice, but the air in the room had definitely changed.

"I was just asking Felicity if she'd like to join us for family dinner tonight."

Felicity's heart leaped into her throat. Then, when she saw the look of utter horror on Austin's face, it plunged into her stomach.

"You did what?" he said.

"You heard me. Dad's out of town. Things will be a little more casual tonight. Why not bring her to dinner? Mom would love to have her join us."

He turned to Felicity and before she even heard what he had to say, one thought flew into her head: *Oh, dear God, just kill me now.*

"Felicity, please allow me to apologize on behalf of my sister. I know you have much more important things to do than to endure a Fortune family dinner." He pinned Savannah with a pointed look. "Believe me, if I had the choice, I wouldn't go tonight."

Felicity was usually pretty good at reading a situation and knowing what to do. But this felt weird, as if she was looking at it as she swam under water with her eyes open. The best thing she could do right now would be to leave. She didn't understand what was happening between Austin and his sister, but he was clearly not happy about Savannah issuing an invitation to dinner. And why had she done that? She hadn't even brought it up until Austin entered the room. Clearly, the invitation was meant to rankle him.

And it had.

This was Felicity's cue to bow out gracefully before things got more awkward. She needed to excuse herself and leave.

"Thank you for thinking of me, Savannah, but I have plans this evening." She glanced at her watch. "In fact, I should leave now so I can get back to the office and button up a few things before I call it a day. Chaz, it was so nice to meet you. I'll probably see both of you at the ball."

Savannah made disappointed noises, but she didn't try to convince her to stay.

Felicity dared a glance at Austin, who was still holding the folder with the signed documents and frowning at a spot somewhere over Felicity's left shoulder.

"If you're finished with that, I'll take it back to the office," she said. It seemed to snap him out of his trance. He handed her the folder.

"All right, you all have a good night."

As she walked to the door, Austin walked with her. She had the feeling he had something to say, and she wasn't sure she wanted to hear it, especially if he was going to take issue with her telling Savannah about their dinner at R'evolution.

*It was a business dinner. I get it. Even if Savannah was waxing on about it being oh so romantic, I didn't join in. Besides, you chose the restaurant.*

"I hope Kevin knows how lucky he is," Austin said in a low voice, his left hand braced on the frame around the elevator.

*Wait. What?*

"I know I've already said this, but it bears repeating. He'd better not mistreat you."

Did he think when she said she had plans tonight that she had a date with Kevin?

She bit her bottom lip as she racked her brain for a way to tell him her plans were actually with Maia, who had just gotten back from her trip and wanted to take her to dinner in appreciation for her taking care of the corgis.

But there was that vibe again. That slight hint of… what? Jealousy?

Maybe she was way off base, but why else would he have such a bad reaction to a guy he'd never met? Yet, the minute his sister suggested he bring her to the family dinner tonight, he acted as if Savannah had suggested he elope with Felicity.

Clearly, Austin didn't want her, but he had a real problem with the thought of Kevin having her.

Maybe it would be good for Austin to stew a little bit.

*Let him think I'm seeing Kevin tonight. It might give him pause and make him take stock of what he wants.*

## Chapter Six

"What the hell is wrong with you, Savannah?" Austin fumed after he walked back into the living room after showing Felicity to the door.

"No, Austin, what the hell is wrong with you?" Savannah countered. "Felicity is a beautiful woman. I was just trying to make it easier on you to ask her out."

Austin gave his head a sharp shake. "You can't just invite someone to Mom and Dad's on a whim like that," he said. "Especially if it's to further this matchmaking game of yours. For your information, I have eyes. I can see that Felicity is a beautiful woman. She's also my assistant. You're barking up the wrong tree. I can't even act remotely interested in her because I'm her boss. Having a little fun with my assistant is a fast track to a sexual harassment lawsuit. Are you trying to bankrupt the family business? Because it sure seems that way."

Savannah shook her head. "I'm not buying it. I think the whole boss-employee thing is a convenient excuse. Because it's not the fact that you aren't interested in her, you're not interested in *anybody* or *anything* except work, and if you're not careful, you're going to work yourself into an early grave. I love you too much to stand by and watch you do that to yourself. You have to stop being such a grump and loosen up. At least allow yourself to have a little fun."

He crossed his arms over his chest, a protective armor. "Are you finished?"

Savannah blinked at him. "No, I'm not finished. Are you kidding?"

"Well, I'm not either," Austin said. "Your 'have fun' prescription is good in theory, but not everyone has the same idea of *fun*."

"Fair enough," Savannah conceded. "What is your idea of fun, then?"

"Well, it's certainly not taking the afternoon off work to fight with my sister. Talk about someone needing to loosen up. Are you playing the role of pot or kettle today?"

Savannah smirked and waved away his question with a flick of her wrist. "Okay, here's my idea of fun: I want to take Chaz to Bourbon Street. He's never seen it. Why don't you come with us and ask Felicity to join you?"

"Did you hear a word I said?" Austin asked.

"I did. And did you hear me say I'm not buying it?

You get this look on your face when you're with her. The chemistry between you is so strong, it should have its own element on the periodic table."

"I think you're mistaking a good working relationship with something romantic. As I said, I can hardly have 'a little fun' with my personal assistant. I'll be real with you—she is the best thing that's ever happened to me, but not in the way you think. It's purely platonic. Besides, she's seeing someone."

He thought of her going out with Kevin Clooney again tonight. What was this, their third or fourth date? Not that he'd been counting. He couldn't help but notice because something seemed to remind him of it every time he turned around.

And he hated it.

Savannah was watching him again, sizing him up. "Do you realize you were in such a good mood until Felicity mentioned that she has plans tonight?"

"No, I was in a good mood until you took it upon yourself to invite her to dinner tonight. You put me in the middle of a very embarrassing situation."

Savannah started to protest again. Austin held up his hand. There was no use in rehashing the same argument again, which was what was about to happen unless he circumnavigated it.

"Would you get off my back and drop this Felicity crusade if I agree to go on a date?"

Savannah's face lit up and her mouth dropped open.

"Not with Felicity," he hastened to add. "I can see what you were thinking. I'll ask someone to go to Bourbon Street with me, you and Chaz. Someone who is not Felicity."

He was going to ask Macks Cole. Why not? He wasn't serious about dating Macks, but essentially, it would serve two purposes: It would allow him to get his sister off his back, and it would be good for client relations.

It was a total win-win.

Why did he feel so empty?

"Your father sends his best wishes." Sarah Fortune glanced around her dining room table, smiling at her children, Austin, Georgia, Belle, Beau, Draper and Savannah. All of her kids were present, except for Nolan, who was in Texas. "Your dad wishes he could be here tonight. Savannah and Chaz, he specifically asked me to reiterate that he is looking forward to spending time with you in a few days when he gets home. This merger he's working on has taken a lot out of him. That and the Charlotte Robinson incidents have him so stressed out, he's wound tighter than a clock."

"He shouldn't worry so much." Savannah said, as she pushed a bite of roast chicken into her peas, sending them tumbling into the untouched mountain of mashed potatoes. "He especially shouldn't worry about the wedding. It will be fine."

"I'm sure it will be beautiful," Sarah said. "I hope Gerald and Deborah will share photos."

"Why photos?" Savannah asked. "You're going, aren't you?"

Austin tried to catch his sister's eye, but she was

transfixed on their mother. He wanted to kick himself for not preparing his sister for this when she came over that afternoon.

Sarah shook her head. "Your father is adamantly opposed to our attending the wedding. Because of everything that's happened, it's just not safe. We decided this at last week's family dinner. I suppose I should've told you sooner, but I knew you were coming for a visit and I thought I'd tell you in person."

Savannah and Chaz exchanged a look.

"What?" asked Sarah. "What was that look about?"

Savannah cleared her throat. "Chaz and I have already RSVP'd that we will be there. It would be rude to back out this close to the wedding, since it's only a month away."

Sarah frowned. "It's six weeks away. There's still plenty of time to send your regrets if you do it soon."

Savannah's mouth pinched into a pucker, a sure sign she was about to deliver news that wouldn't please their mother. "I understand your concern, but if I can live through my apartment being vandalized and still feel brave enough to go, I'd hope my immediate family could be courageous enough to come with me and support our extended family."

Sarah flinched, and Austin knew it was time to step in.

"Savannah," Austin said, "we understand where you're coming from, but I hope you'll listen to what we have to say. It's important."

"So, our family has sides now? All of you against Chaz and me?"

"Don't be that way," Austin said. "Charlotte Robinson has proven herself to be a dangerous woman who will stop at nothing to get revenge on the Fortunes. The divorce from Gerald and his upcoming wedding to Deborah have no doubt set her off and made her bitter toward our entire family. I think we haven't heard the last from her. I believe she's not going to stop until she makes a big statement, and what better place to do that than at her ex-husband's wedding?"

Savannah made a dubious sound. "Well, I believe they're going to catch her before the wedding. We've already talked about this, Austin. I don't understand why you're doing an about-face now."

"Talked about what?" Sarah asked.

Savannah turned back to her mother. "I forgot to tell you this last night, but I mentioned it to Austin earlier today. Kate Fortune is sick of Charlotte's shenanigans and she has made it her mission to put an end to all the craziness. She is determined to find the woman and see her arrested and locked up. I'll bet that Charlotte will be in jail by the time the wedding rolls around. I mean with Kate on it, you know it's bound to happen. And you know Gerald isn't just huddled in a corner quaking with fear. Not when his wedding is on the line. You know he's got to be doing everything he can to make sure his wedding day isn't ruined."

"She's not behind bars yet," Sarah said. "I wouldn't be surprised if she laid low until the wedding, so she could go out with a bang."

"Okay, I'll make a deal with you," Savannah said.

"If Charlotte is still on the loose by the time the wedding happens next month, I won't go."

"What are you going to do?" Beau asked. "Just not show up? That's worse than canceling now. If you bowed out now, at least you'd give them a chance to notify the caterer and they won't get stuck paying for your meal."

Belle narrowed her eyes. "I think Savannah has a point. Do you really think Gerald will go through with the wedding if Charlotte is still on the loose?"

No one answered. Even though Gerald was their half uncle, they really didn't know him very well. What they did know had come from news stories about how he had grown his garage-based computer company in to a billion-dollar empire. Though Gerald was a self-made man like their dad, Miles Fortune preferred to keep a more private profile. Another way the half brothers differed was that Gerald appeared to be a cutthroat business mogul who looked out for only himself, or, at least, that's the way the media had painted him.

It was difficult to know whether or not the guy would look out for the greater good and postpone his wedding if Charlotte was still at large.

"Have you ever considered that Charlotte is terrorizing us right now?" Savannah countered. "She has us living scared, ready to give up something we want to do because we are frightened of her. If we don't go, we're playing right into her hands. She will have won."

"Sounds like we're damned if we do and damned if we don't," said Draper. "If we don't go, she'll win by keeping us away. If we do go and she manages to blow us all up, she'll win and we will die."

Sarah shoved her chair back from the table. The sound of the wood scraping the floor echoed in the dining room as she stood. "I don't want to talk about this anymore," she demanded. "It's far too upsetting. It's not often that I have most of my children together. I am not going to let that crazy woman rob me of this night. So, I'm going into the kitchen to get dessert. When I come back, let's please talk about something more pleasant. While I'm gone, would someone clear the table and make room for the next course?"

After their mother left the room, Draper and Georgia stood and started moving the dinner plates to a tray on a stand positioned next to the sideboard. The other siblings sat in stunned silence amid the sound of clinking china and flatware.

Finally, Beau brought his hands together in a single clap. "Well, that was fun."

Austin shot his brother a look. "Mom and Dad have decided that the family is going to sit this one out," he said.

Savannah pounded her flat palms on the table. "What makes them think they can speak for us?" she asked. "The last time I checked, we were adults. I'm sorry that they'll be disappointed, but Chaz and I are going to the wedding whether they like it or not. We are adults—as are each and every one of you. Mom and Dad need to understand that they don't get to make decisions for us anymore."

Austin's mind bounced back to Felicity and his tangled feelings that were wrapped around Fortune Investments' no-fraternizing policy and the debacle of all that had happened with his marriage and subsequent divorce. He wasn't letting his parents decide whether or not he could explore a more personal relationship with Felicity.

He had weighed both sides. On the one side, Fortune Investment could lose a good employee and potentially get slapped with a harassment suit, though that didn't seem like Felicity's style. On the other side were all these strange feelings that had suddenly stirred in his heart after all these years. With Kelly, he had jumped before he weighed all the dangers. Not anymore. This time the negatives weighed heavier than the positives, warning him that getting involved with Felicity would end badly for everyone.

Sarah returned with a mile-high chocolate cake. "Will someone help me, please, and get the coffee while I serve the cake?"

Savannah and Austin both stood. Without another word, they walked into the kitchen. "I can't wait to get out of here and go to the French Quarter before I say or do irreparable damage to my relationship with Mom. She is so freaked out about this. But the parents and I are going to have to agree to disagree on this because I'm going to the wedding."

"So, you're set on going, then?" Austin asked.

It wasn't optimal, but he was confident enough in the strength of their family bond to know that even if Savannah did break rank and attend the wedding, her relationship with their parents might be strained for a while but the family bond wouldn't be broken. In fact, there was very little any of them could do to cause that kind of damage. Their bond was that strong.

Savannah nodded. "We can't live scared, Austin. Otherwise, it's not much of a life. You could apply the same philosophy to your dating life. You can't let Kelly keep you from finding love. Otherwise, she wins in a big way. Even though you say you have no feelings for her, essentially, she's holding your heart hostage. You need to adopt my credo and refuse to negotiate with terrorists, which essentially describes Kelly, and absolutely describes Charlotte."

"Yeah, well, let's leave my dating life out of this," he said. "Kelly is not holding my heart hostage. Just as you draw boundaries with Mom, I've drawn them with Kelly. And now I'm drawing them with you."

He smiled at her in a way that showed he meant business but that he wasn't mad at her. Savannah had always been a feisty one. Austin resisted the urge to ask her how often she'd been in the position to negotiate with terrorists, as she'd put it. He also curbed the urge to ask her why she was so hell-bent on attending the wedding of this newfound family member at the risk of upsetting her immediate family, but that would only get her more riled up and make her more determined to go.

"We'll see how it goes," Austin said, realizing the generalization could apply to both the Charlotte situation and his dating life. "In the meantime, let's eat dessert in peace, so we can leave things on good terms with mom. Then you can blow off some steam on Bourbon Street. I can't stay long because I have a long day tomorrow."

"But you're still bringing a date tonight, right?" Savannah asked, as she poured coffee into cups on a tray. "I'm not pressuring you. But you did say you would."

"I don't know that I'd call her a *date*. She's more of a business acquaintance, but that's one of the reasons I came into the kitchen. I am going to call her now."

Savannah's eyes lit up. "If calling her a business acquaintance makes you feel better, go for it. I'm proud of you for putting yourself out there. Though, if I'm completely honest, I wish you would've asked Felicity. I just like you two together. Your chemistry lights up a room."

Austin shrugged. Even if he wanted to ask Felicity to join them, he couldn't. "Felicity has plans tonight."

"That's too bad." Savannah lifted the tray. "It just goes to show you. If you snooze, you lose. But I'll get out of here, so you can make your call."

She bumped open the kitchen door with her backside, leaving him alone to phone Macks. He dialed her number before he could change his mind. She answered on the fourth ring, just as Austin had begun to anticipate the call sailing over to voice mail.

"This is Macks." Her tone was brusque.

"Hello, Macks. It's Austin Fortune."

"Well, hello there, Austin Fortune. To what do I owe this wonderful surprise?"

Her tone had changed. Where it had been all business and efficiency when she'd answered the phone, now she was virtually purring warmth and enthusiasm. Maybe this wasn't such a good idea after all. But it was too late to change his mind now.

"I know this is last-minute, but my sister and her boyfriend are in town. Chaz has never seen Bourbon Street. We are heading down there this evening for a drink, and I wanted to invite you to join us."

The silence on the other end of the line lasted so long, he wondered if they'd lost their connection.

"Bourbon Street? Thank you for thinking of me, but no. I don't think so, Austin. That's not really my scene."

Not her scene? He bit back a laugh. As if it was anyone's *scene*. Bourbon Street was a rite of passage, a been-there-done-that sort of thing you checked off the list, or something you endured when visitors came to town and they wanted to see it, which was the case with Chaz. For a split second, Austin was tempted to tell her as much, but it just felt exhausting. Bourbon Street certainly wasn't his scene, and, he realized, someone as seemingly high maintenance as Macks wasn't either.

Since his divorce, he'd found dating in general to take too much time and energy. But, he reminded himself, he wasn't trying to date Macks. She was a business acquaintance, and that alone helped him keep his retort to himself.

"I completely understand. Have a nice evening, Macks."

"Oh, Austin," she said before she could disconnect the call. "Did you get a chance to consider the invitation I gave to Felicity for you? It's to the opening of a show for one of my clients."

"Felicity mentioned it, but I was out of the office and

didn't get a chance to look at the details. I will when I am at my desk tomorrow, and I will let you know."

"That sounds wonderful, darling," she purred. "I do hope you can make it. I'd love to see you. Just not on Bourbon Street."

As Maia drained the pasta, Felicity refilled their wineglasses waiting atop the kitchen island. Maia's three corgis, Honey, Buddy and Jasmine, played in the living room, which was visible from the kitchen of the open concept house.

"Start from the beginning and tell me everything," Maia insisted.

Felicity did a quick rundown of everything that had happened since Kevin had sent her flowers.

"To me, it sounds like Austin is jealous," Maia said. "That means you either need to tell him how you feel, or you need to put him in the past."

As if it were that easy. She would've forgotten about Austin a long time ago if she could.

"Let me back up," Maia said. "Do you like Kevin? Because it sure sounds like he likes you."

Kevin was fine. But did she like him? That was a loaded question. She certainly didn't have anything against him. Although, at times he came across a little pushy. He kept saying he wanted to pick her up at the office and take her somewhere. She didn't want him to come to the office because if he did, judging by the way Austin had been acting, Austin might not like it very much.

On one hand, why shouldn't she be able to have

dates pick her up at the office? As long as it was after hours and didn't interfere with her work. Austin had no business telling her what she could and couldn't do with her own time. And Macks had brought that invitation to the office for him. Granted, he wasn't there, and Felicity had no idea what was going on between the two of them—

"Hello! Felicity, where did you go?"

"I'm here. I have a lot on my mind."

"Stay present, girlfriend. You spend too much time in your head. *Kevin*. I asked you if you like Kevin. Because if you like him, you are going to lose him if you keep mooning over the Beast, who I don't think is nearly good enough for you."

Felicity rolled her eyes. Of course Maia would think that. To say she wasn't fond of Austin was an understatement.

"You are acting as if this is my final answer. As if I have to commit or lose out on love for the rest of my life. I am not ready to choose right now. I like Kevin—as in he is a perfectly nice guy. I am not in love with Kevin, and I'm certainly not at a place where I am going to forsake all others for him."

"I didn't say you had to do that. I just don't want him to get frustrated with you."

"Did you ever consider that if Kevin is that impatient, maybe he's not the guy for me?"

Maia offered Felicity a conceding one-shoulder shrug.

"All I can say is I'm not in a place to commit to anyone and I don't know if or when I will be."

Felicity's thoughts drifted back to the evening at R'evolution and the easy conversation with Austin. She wasn't ready to share that with Maia. Because for all of her friend's good intentions, she did tend to take things out of context and run with them. In Maia's world, a romantic dinner could only mean that Austin was interested and therefore Felicity should bear her soul. But if she tacked on Macks Cole and included what happened this afternoon at Austin's condo, when Savannah's invitation had pushed Austin back into his shell, Maia's cut-and-dried interpretation would be that she should forget him.

Felicity only wished she could. Because life would be so much easier.

## Chapter Seven

Felicity sensed Austin approaching before he got to her desk. It was funny how she could do that. It was as if she had a sixth sense and could feel his energy before she even saw him or heard him approaching.

This morning he was walking with a white envelope or card in his hands. It was the same size and shape of the one Macks had dropped off. A sense of dread lodged in her stomach.

"Sorry to interrupt. Would you please put the art show that Macks Cole invited me to on my calendar?"

He handed her the card.

"Sure. Happy to." *Liar.* "Would you like me to make a dinner reservation for two before the show?"

He squinted at her as if she had asked him a question in a foreign language. "A dinner reservation? No.

That's not necessary. Most likely, I'm just going to drop in as a courtesy."

*A courtesy?* That was very encouraging. She would take him being courteous to Macks over him having a date with her anytime.

As she called up Austin's calendar to add the date, the dread that had weighed down her insides a moment ago changed to something much lighter that she couldn't quite identify, but it wasn't bad.

"When I talked to her last night, I told her I'd stop by. The show is at her gallery. She wouldn't have time to go to dinner."

And just like that, the not-so-bad feeling was smashed by the wrecking ball that swung through her middle.

So, they talked last night. *How cozy.*

She took care to keep a neutral expression on her face. She certainly didn't need to give herself away now, even if she was feeling crushed by disappointment. She didn't know why she felt the need to test the waters further. But she did.

"I don't recall Macks's name being on the invitation list for the gala. Should I send her an invitation?"

Austin seemed to consider her question for a moment.

"No, don't send her an invitation. That seems too formal. I'll ask her myself."

Austin had no idea why he'd said he would ask Macks to the ball when he had no intention of doing so. Actually, that was a lie. He had wanted to see if Felicity would react.

As he sat down at his desk, he scrubbed his eyes with his palms. She'd offered no reaction. Sure, he was going to stop by the gallery, but he had never even been on a date with Macks. The one time he'd asked her to get together, she had made it clear that she liked things on her own terms. The last thing he needed to worry about at something as important as the FI charity gala was a high-maintenance date. For a moment he regretted not having Felicity send Macks an invitation to attend on her own. The woman had money and he would be remiss in turning down her donation for their charity, much less the cost of a ticket. Maybe he would hand deliver the invitation himself, just as Macks had delivered the invitation to the art opening. She could bring her own date, just not him.

When Kevin called, he'd caught Felicity at a weak moment. He'd texted her about an hour after she'd put Macks's art event on Austin's calendar and had been stewing on the thought of Austin taking Macks to the ball. It was one thing to think, in abstract, of Austin dating Macks, but to have to watch them together at an event she had to attend… Well, that sounded like cruel and unusual punishment. Utter torture.

That's why when Kevin asked her to go to dinner that evening she said yes. On any other night she would've declined. But tonight, she had absolutely nothing going on, except plans to brood over Austin's interest in Macks. And how next to gorgeous, willowy, sophisticated Macks, Felicity felt like a hairy chimp—despite having every waxable region of her body serviced.

So, in a split second, she'd weighed the pros and cons of seeing Kevin tonight. And now he was picking her up at the office at 6:30.

She stole a surreptitious glance at Austin and her heart melted a little. She couldn't help it. His hair was a little longer than it should be because a meeting had preempted the hair appointment she'd made for him and he'd said he was too busy this week. But his hair was exactly the length she liked because after he raked his hands through it, as was his habit when he was focusing on something important, it got mussed and she'd decided that's exactly what he would look like when he woke up first thing in the morning. Felicity blinked away the thought, smiling secretly to herself. He was wearing a blue shirt and a navy tie. It was a great color on him. But, come to think of it, had she really seen him in a color that didn't look good?

*Your sister approves of me, even if you don't think of me as anything more than an employee.*

That's when he suddenly looked up and caught her in a full-on mooning daydream. She was too deep in her trance to look away quickly before he caught her. So, he caught her staring at him, with her elbow on her desk and her cheek resting on her hand. The only thing missing from the picture was her doodling his name on a notebook while cartoon hearts and flowers danced over her head.

He gave her a little wave, which was humiliating, and, of course, meant to convey that he had caught her daydreaming. The thing about Austin, though, was that he would never call her out for slacking off. Even if it appeared that she was coasting for a moment or two, she knew he knew her work ethic and respected the fact that she worked long, hard hours and was dedicated to her job. Still, it didn't quell the embarrassment of being caught in the act of staring at him. She figured it was the perfect time to go to the restroom and fix her makeup. Kevin would be there to pick her up in about twenty minutes.

Austin was still watching her when she stood up from her desk. She grabbed her purse and gave him a little wave that echoed the one he'd offered a moment ago. He smiled at her and laughed a little in a way that seemed an awful lot like flirting. With the exception of his mild freak-out yesterday when Savannah had invited her to their family dinner, Austin's mood had seemed lighter lately.

*Probably because he's in love…even if he doesn't know it.*

Because wasn't that what happened to a person when they fell in love? It transformed the way they looked at the world, the way they treated others. No wonder he didn't want her to come to the dinner last night. How in the world would he explain her presence at an intimate family gathering to Macks? Or maybe he'd invited her to the dinner. He'd said he'd talked to her last night. Maybe he was taking her home to meet the family? But his father was out of town. It seemed like he might wait…unless Miles had already met her.

She was a prospective client of Fortune Investments, after all.

Felicity sighed. Her heart felt heavy as she made her way down the silent hallway to the ladies room. Since it was creeping up on 6:30, most of the employees had already gone home. She and Austin were two of the only people in the office.

She studied her reflection in the mirror. Her cheeks were flushed—probably from the lingering embarrassment caused by Austin catching her staring. She smoothed her cream-colored top down over her black pants. It wasn't what she would've chosen to wear if she'd had advance notice of a date, but it was good enough for tonight.

She pulled her cosmetics bag out of her purse. Before the makeover Maia had given her, she hadn't worried about touching up her makeup and hadn't carried a cosmetics bag in her purse. But since Austin had noticed her haircut, and of course, since Macks had waltzed onto the scene, it had become her armor.

Now she was glad she'd taken Maia up on the offer to find her a dress to wear for the ball. Maia did hair and makeup for beauty pageant contestants, and she was certain one of her pageant girls would be willing to lend a dress. Maia was like a dog with a tug toy when she set her mind to something like this. There would be no putting her off, no talking her out of it. Frankly, Felicity wasn't about to ask her to stand down. She wanted the brightest, shiniest, most pageant-y gown Maia could find. She wanted Austin to look at her and think, there she is, Miss Fricking America.

Or at least in theory that's what she wanted. She wanted him, despite the fact that she was too paralyzed to let herself take steps to make that a reality. Or maybe she fancied herself in love with him because he was unavailable—or at least not available to her.

She owed her love-related post-traumatic stress to her parents and their nasty divorce, a debacle that had left her mother alone and broken after the love of her life had walked out and left her high and dry for a woman fifteen years his junior.

Watching her mother suffer had left such a scar on Felicity that she would rather pine over a guy who was unattainable than give herself a chance with a guy like Kevin, who was interested enough in her that he was willing to look past her tepid reception of his attention and keep pursuing her.

The thing was, Felicity believed in love. She believed in love in a big way. She felt it every day, every time she looked at or thought of Austin. The problem was, she also knew that love that intense never lasted. It was like a match. In its purest, unused form, it held all the possibility in the world. However, once struck and ignited, it was only a matter of time until it burned itself out to a worthless nothing.

As she powdered her nose, touched up her bronzer and reapplied her lipstick, she made a promise to herself that she was going to give Kevin a chance tonight. She would force herself to give him her attention and not let her mind wander to Austin. She wouldn't ponder the coincidental timing of Austin's interest in Macks— after the flowers from Kevin had arrived for Felicity.

She wouldn't let herself sit there with Kevin and wonder if it been a huge mistake to let Austin know she was playing the dating game. That would assume Austin had feelings for her, too, because why else would he get jealous? She wouldn't ponder what might happen if she went for broke and confessed her feelings to Austin since she was leaving Fortune Investments after graduation. No. Dinner the other night would've been the perfect time to do that.

It seemed pretty clear that ship had sailed.

As Felicity was putting away her makeup, her phone sounded a text message. It was from Kevin saying he'd be there in five minutes and asking if he could come in and visit the restroom. He'd tacked on a comment that it would be a good chance to see where she spent so much of her time.

I want to see if it matches the mental picture I have when I think of you at work.

Since Austin was still here, Felicity hesitated. She knew it wasn't a good idea to let Kevin come up, but it wouldn't be very nice to deny him the restroom.

Austin caught the movement out of the corner of his eye. When he looked up, he saw a guy who looked vaguely familiar standing at Felicity's desk. All of a sudden, everything snapped into place.

*Kevin Clooney.*

That's why the guy's name sounded so familiar. He'd met Kevin Clooney before. About a year ago, one of the New Orleans television stations had sponsored a hometown version of the show *Shark Tank* to match up local entrepreneurs with possible venture capitalists. Austin had been one of the financiers. He had been flattered to be invited to be part of a panel that would hear pitches and possibly strike deals with the budding business creatives. He was jazzed at the thought of possibly having a hand in making someone's dreams come true.

Of course, it had to be the right project.

He'd heard Kevin Clooney's pitch. Sadly, it hadn't been a very good one. He might have thought his idea for the *Skin to Win* burlesque food truck had sounded titillating, but it wasn't viable for many reasons. The biggest reason was, even in New Orleans, the type of show Kevin wanted to produce alongside his food truck didn't comply with city ordinances.

When Austin had questioned him on what elements of burlesque he was thinking of—the exaggerated comedic angle or the striptease version—Kevin had indicated "all of the above." When Austin told him it wouldn't fly, the guy proceeded to argue with Austin, saying that it would be in the same vein as the antics that happen during Mardi Gras, to which Austin replied, that despite its bawdy reputation, the city was trying tried very hard to keep Mardi Gras as clean as possible.

Austin finally shut him down by saying he wasn't interested in investing. It wasn't the type of business the Fortunes wanted associated with their name. Period. Kevin Clooney had called Austin a prude. As if insulting him was going to make him reconsider and fund the guy's unworthy project.

Did Felicity know about Kevin's striptease food truck idea?

Of course, a lot could change in a year. Maybe the guy had learned some manners, even though Austin didn't believe it.

When Kevin Clooney saw Austin watching him, he waved. If Austin hadn't been pissed off before, he was now. But this was his moment to let the guy know he remembered him and he still wasn't impressed with what he saw.

Why was Felicity even talking to this dude?

Austin walked out to Felicity's desk, where she appeared to be hurrying Kevin out of the office. Purse on her arm, she looked a little sheepish when Austin approached them.

"Austin Fortune." He extended a hand.

Felicity should've stuck to her guns and met Kevin downstairs, despite his need for the bathroom.

She knew that now.

"We've met," Kevin said in his overly enthusiastic wheeler-dealer tone as he accepted Austin's hand and clapped him on the back. "Austin, my man, don't crush me and say you don't remember me. I'm Kevin Clooney."

"I remember you, Kevin. You're hard to forget."

Kevin laughed, obviously taking Austin's words as a compliment. Felicity, however, could read her boss and could sense the waves of irritation rippling off him.

Austin glanced at Felicity and furrowed his brow. She frowned and bit her bottom lip, trying to telepath an apology.

"It's good to see you again, man," Kevin said, as if he was Austin's long lost best friend.

Austin didn't reply to him. Instead he turned to her. "Felicity, don't forget we have the final walk through at the Roosevelt Hotel tomorrow evening."

This time Felicity was the one to arch a brow at him. She knew he'd just come up with this fieldtrip because it wasn't on the calendar. "Of course," she said. "How could I forget?"

"We are preparing for the Fortune Investment charity gala, Kevin," Austin said. "This is an important event for our family foundation. Felicity has been instrumental in organizing the event for the past several years. It keeps her very busy."

This was obviously for Kevin's benefit. Austin was blocking off her schedule and making sure Kevin knew it. She wasn't sure which irritated her more, Kevin's aggressive approach or Austin's passive aggressiveness. Either way, she hated being stuck in the middle.

"Cool. So, Austin, I have another business proposition I want to run by you. Can I get on your schedule this week?"

Felicity fumed. The guy really was obtuse.

"Kevin, we need to go," she said.

"As I just said," Austin interjected, "I'm slammed until after the gala and even after that I'm pretty sure I'm booked."

"It'll only take a minute. It's an opportunity I know

you won't want to miss. I'm sure Felicity could fit me in. Let me buy you breakfast. Ya gotta eat."

"Actually, I have to make a call." Austin pinned Felicity with a pointed look and turned around and walked away.

"But, hey, if you're busy, I get it," Kevin called out. "I'll be in touch. Talk soon."

Felicity was silent as Kevin talked nonstop in the elevators down to the first floor. Once they were outside, she stopped in front of the doors.

"Kevin, did you come inside so you could pitch your business idea to Austin?"

"I came inside to pick you up for our date, like any gentleman would do." He was being prickly. Maybe he wasn't as obtuse as Felicity had thought. "I had no idea that he would be in the office. But he was, so I took the opportunity. Don't tell me you're mad. How can you be mad at that?"

She wasn't mad. She was furious. She had to take a minute to collect herself so she didn't go off on him.

Kevin filled the silence. In what she was beginning to recognize as true Kevin Clooney fashion, his reaction was dramatic and completely unapologetic. "Not everyone is as fortunate as the almighty Fortunes. I won't apologize for being ambitious. I bet if you went back to the days before Miles Fortune made his money, he probably had to stick his neck out and take opportunities when he could get them, too. And then you have Austin Fortune—"

*Don't say it. Do not talk about Austin. Do not even hint that he was handed everything.*

"The guy was born holding the silver spoon—"

Felicity snapped. "Do not talk about Austin. I have seen few people work as hard as he does. So, don't even go there. The guy hardly has a life outside of this building."

"Look, don't get salty. I am not doubting that the guy works hard. What I was going to say was, you'd think a guy who was born into privilege—" Kevin held out his hand like a traffic cop, effectively stopping Felicity from interrupting "—because he was born into it—good, bad, or whatever, you can't dispute that fact. I'd think that if he had any decency, he would want to pay his good fortune forward. Any decent person would."

"Look—" Felicity started, but Kevin's hand went out again and it was starting to annoy her.

"All I'm saying is the best way he could pay it forward would be to help an ambitious, hardworking businessperson like me."

Felicity put her hands on her hips. "I am going to ask you one thing, Kevin, and I want you to tell me the truth. And then we are not going to mention Austin again tonight, or I am going to turn around and walk away. Do you understand me?"

Kevin nodded and looked slightly annoyed. "What's your question?"

"Why didn't you tell me you'd met Austin before?"

Kevin's brows knit. "Because you never asked?"

Tired of his patronizing tone, she turned around and walked away.

"Felicity, come back. I'm sorry. It's a good thing I

didn't mention it since it seems to piss you off when I do talk about him."

Felicity whirled around. "Let's get a couple of things straight, Kevin. First, Austin Fortune—or any of the Fortunes, for that matter—do not owe you anything. They are decent people who give back more than their fair share to their community. And the other thing is, you will not use me to get to my boss. That's what pisses me off."

Kevin gave her the big-eyed innocent look, which made Felicity even more mad. Body Language 101.

"I think it's best for us to call it a night," she said.

She turned to walk to her car.

"You really want to know why I didn't tell you?"

Felicity kept walking.

"Let's go get some dinner and I'll tell you why I didn't mention I knew your boss."

When Felicity hesitated, he said, "If it makes you feel better, you can drive yourself and leave whenever you want. But please hear me out."

## Chapter Eight

The next morning, Austin got into the office earlier than usual, even before Felicity, which had happened maybe three or four times since she had been working for him. Last night, he hadn't been able to sleep thinking about what had transpired in the office right before Felicity had left for the day.

He had tossed and turned, debating whether or not he should sit Felicity down and tell her exactly what Kevin Clooney was all about, or at least Austin's perception of the guy. And in all fairness, being ambitious wasn't a crime. Austin knew that.

However, he wanted to make sure Felicity knew Kevin's game so she could make sure the guy wasn't just using her as an entrée into Fortune Investments. But that sounded smug, even to his own ears. God, it even sounded disrespectful. She was a beautiful woman. Clearly, access to Fortune Investments financing wasn't the only reason Kevin was interested in her. And that was a problem. If Felicity was dating the guy, it meant that she was taken. Austin would never know if his feelings for her were real or if they had sprung from the very real fact that he couldn't have her.

He wanted her to be happy.

She was the best thing that had ever happened to him. Felicity had been working for a temp agency and had come to Fortune Investments to help him out on a temporary basis. He'd been a wreck. His life had been a mess after things had fallen apart with Kelly. He needed someone to help him get his act together, because he couldn't even think straight after the divorce.

The minute Felicity walked in, not only did she have an instant calming effect on him, but she had also been damn good at what she did: untangling his life and freeing up his mind so that he could focus on what he did best—make money for Fortune Investments. God knew he had no choice but to work his ass off because he'd had to pay back his father for the financial hole that Kelly had left him in. Which brought him full circle.

Since Kelly, Felicity had been the only person outside of his family he had allowed himself to trust. He trusted her without a doubt. So, he was certain when it came to Kevin Clooney, she would protect the interests of Fortune Investments.

But when it came to matters of the heart…that was a little unclear.

About a half hour later, Felicity arrived. Austin stood. He had already decided that it would be best just to rip the bandage off and go out and talk to her, rather than letting things sit and fester. "Good morning," he said.

"Good morning." She looked like she'd had about the same quality of sleep as he had. "Austin, I'm so sorry about yesterday." Her voice shook, and his heart clenched at the sound of it. He hated to see her look so torn up, but he also needed to make sure she understood why he'd acted toward Kevin the way he had.

"Do you want to come into my office and talk?" he offered.

"I do." Her voice was soft, and she looked subdued as she twisted in her chair, then stood.

Today, she was wearing a pale yellow dress that made him think of sunshine. He wished this dark cloud would pass and the sun would come out again. In due time.

"Austin, I didn't know that Kevin had met you before, and I certainly didn't know he had pitched you a business idea in the past. If I had known, I wouldn't have let him pick me up at work. He was the one who suggested it, because I told him I needed to work late. But I told him that going forward, any talk about business would have to go through you. There will be no suggesting that I slide him onto your schedule, unless you tell me to slide him on."

"Does that mean you're going to keep seeing him?" Austin knew he had no right to ask.

He was edging into dangerous territory, but at the moment, he didn't give a damn.

Felicity blinked. "I don't know."

Austin blinked. "Either you are or you aren't going to see him. It's a simple question." *Dammit*. He could hear his tone, but the feelings inside him were like a living beast trying to get out.

She stared at him with wide brown eyes. So much for showing her the softer side of himself.

"Why do you need to know that, Austin?" she asked. "Is there a reason? Is there something you want to say to me?"

He scrubbed his hand over his face. There was so much he wanted to say to her. So much he wanted to do. He wanted to pull her up from the chair, straight into his arms and taste those lips that were going to be the death of him if he didn't get to taste them soon.

But he couldn't do that anymore than he could demand to know if she intended to keep seeing Kevin Clooney or forbid her from seeing him again.

"What is there to say?" he asked.

She shook her head. "I have no idea. You are confusing me, Austin."

That's because he was confused. He had no idea what these feelings were or where they came from. The best thing he could do was change the subject.

"Look, I know you well enough to know you would never do anything that would put Fortune Investments in jeopardy. I have to be judicious with the investment proposals that I bring to the board. I don't want Kevin pressuring you to get to me, when I don't even know if I can help him. That's why I need to know if you're going to continue seeing him."

Felicity nodded, and Austin thought he glimpsed disappointment in her eyes. He couldn't make sense of it. She didn't even seem to like the guy.

"Kevin is purchasing a table at the foundation gala."

"Why?" Austin asked.

Felicity frowned at him. "Why does anyone buy a table at a charity event like this, Austin? He's doing it to support your family's foundation. You can't very well turn him away. Besides, I'm the one who will be making the biggest sacrifice. His stipulation for buying the table was that I would be his date to the gala."

"You should've said no."

"Well, I didn't. And you can at least act decent and grateful about it."

Her words were a punch to the gut. Austin regarded her for a moment. Then he straightened, pulling himself together. "You're right. If he wants to contribute to the cause, we'll gladly take his check. But you do not have to be his date. That's a slimy stipulation to attach to a charity donation."

Felicity shrugged. "Of course, I told him that I would be up and down from the table because I'll be working that night."

Austin's eyes widened, and he smiled conspiratorially. "Yeah, unfortunately, I think you're going to be pretty darn busy that night."

"You realize it means you'll have to be nice to him, right?" She smiled, but her words were one hundred percent the truth.

"Of course, I'll be on my best behavior." He smiled,

too, but he wasn't sure it reached his eyes. She looked at him for a moment, as if she wanted to say something.

"What's on your mind?" he asked.

She shook her head.

"No, tell me. After all these years one of the best things about you and me is that we can be real with each other."

"All right, you really want to know?"

He nodded.

"I was thinking that you can be a real piece of work."

"Well, you know me better than most people. So, it's probably true."

She laughed, and it sounded like music.

Another good thing about them was that even when they disagreed, they always tried to leave things in a good place. Married couples could borrow that page from their playbook. For a moment, his future flashed before his eyes. The two of them, married, with the kids, the dog, the house with the white picket fence. Felicity in his bed every night. Her face would be the last thing he saw when he went to sleep at night and the first thing he saw when he opened his eyes in the morning. Kevin was not part of that picture—

"Don't forget, you have Macks Cole's art show opening tonight."

"Right, but first I have an appointment with my father to talk about creating an advertising position. Do you know anyone who might be interested?"

It had been a long day and Felicity was glad to be home. After the date with Kevin, she had barely slept because she'd been afraid Austin would tell her Fortune Investments no longer needed her services. He couldn't fire her because she'd already given her notice, but he could've made her notice effective immediately.

Instead, he'd caught her off guard and shared the news that he was talking to Miles about her promotion. The guy was full of surprises. Especially when he'd said the part about *the best thing about you and me…* Her breath caught again, the same way it had when he'd said the words. She reveled in the idea that he thought in terms of *you and me*. That in his mind, there was an *Austin and Felicity* category.

That's why her heart belonged to him, because, well, he was Austin. Despite his quirky ways and his dark moods, she knew his heart was in the right place—if not exactly in the place she wanted it.

Kevin, on the other hand, was a strange puzzle. Just when she thought she was ready to write him off, he surprised her. When she'd pressed him, he told her he had met Austin before and that Austin had turned down his business proposal. Everything he said matched up with what Austin said, but Felicity found it troublesome that she'd had to ask.

He hadn't volunteered the information. Felicity's gut was telling her that he wouldn't have told her if she hadn't asked. But he had to know that she would find out when he finally came face-to-face with Austin.

Still, even though she realized the connection when Kevin spoke to Austin, he had managed to get in front of him again—for what it was worth. If he'd told Felicity about the connection, she would've never let him come up.

It cast a pall on the evening. Felicity had considered calling it off even before the date started. Then Kevin played the FI charity ball card. He would buy a table if Felicity went out with him and would be his fate to the gala. So, she took one for the team and tried her hardest to make the most of the evening.

The gala was right around the corner. She didn't have to see him again after that. And she shouldn't because her heart just wasn't in it.

How could it be when it belonged to someone else?

Someone else who had a date with another woman this evening. The thought of Austin with beautiful Macks made her stomach queasy. The best thing she could do would be to keep busy.

Felicity looked out the window and saw Maia's car in the driveway. She let herself out the back of her duplex and knocked on Maia's door. Through the French door, she could see Maia wave her in. The phone was pressed to her ear and she appeared to be talking to someone about hair color.

"Candice, I'm sorry you aren't happy with the color," Maia said. "When you asked me to blend your gray with the rest of your hair, I thought you meant you wanted an overall gray look. You know that's very trendy right now. We could even put a lavender tint on it and you'd look very chic."

Maia flinched and held the phone away from her ear. "Candice—Candice—" She rolled her eyes and motioned for Felicity to sit down.

Felicity had the urge to grab the phone and tell Candice to be quiet and let Maia make it right. She would, which was exactly the reason Felicity was there to talk to her.

"Candice, listen to me, please. If you're unhappy. I'm happy to fix it. No charge. I want you to be happy, Candice. I was just offering you options by suggesting the lavender—I understand. Yes. Right. I hear you. Why don't you come in tomorrow at nine o'clock and I'll get you all fixed up?"

Maia could be pushy and act like a mother hen, but she didn't have a mean bone in her body. Even before Felicity had a chance to ask her what she came to ask, she knew the answer. Still, she needed to ask. After she got the answer she knew she'd get, she needed to vent.

"Do you remember mentioning to Kevin that I work for Fortune Investments?"

Maia frowned. "Why?"

Felicity relayed last night's happenings to her friend.

Maia closed her eyes and for a moment she looked as if she might implode.

"Don't hate me. We did talk about you working for the Fortunes. It was only in the name of me trying to fix the two of you up. I wanted him to know you had a good job, that you're successful. I had no idea that he was working an angle. That's just not right and I'm going to tell him that the next time I see him. Unless you want me to call him right now."

Maia punched her pass code into her phone.

"No, Maia, don't. I'm not mad at you. I just needed to know if it was some kind of a crazy coincidence or if Kevin purposely targeted me. I'd say it's kind of half and half. You wanted to fix us up—that's the coincidence half. He got interested in getting to know me after he found out I worked for the Fortunes." Felicity shrugged.

"That little—" Maia called him a colorful word. "I don't appreciate being used. I don't fix up people very often, because when I do and it doesn't work out or if it does work out and they have a breakup—or if something weird like this happens—" She threw her hands in the air. "I feel bad."

"You shouldn't feel bad," Felicity insisted. "This isn't your fault. I shouldn't have told you, but I wanted to get to the bottom of it. Make sure I had the full story."

Felicity followed Maia into the kitchen.

"How did the Beast take it?" Maia asked. "Was he mad at you?"

Felicity shrugged. "He wasn't happy, but in true Austin form after he went off about Kevin, he surprised me by saying that he'd finally pinned down a time to talk to his father about creating that advertising position for me."

Maia's mouth gaped. "And?"

"I don't know. I mean, it's not definite. I didn't see him after the meeting. That probably means that he doesn't have any news for me. I'd think Miles would want to interview me before he offered me the position. But it's way early for that. Austin just broached the conversation today."

Maia laughed the sort of dry, humorless laugh she usually saved for conversations about Austin. She had busied herself in the kitchen, measuring water into a pan and setting it on the stove to boil.

"What's funny?" Felicity asked.

"I just think it's ironic that you say you're leaving, and he tries to create a position to make you stay. He finds out you're dating someone, and he starts acting even more beastly than usual."

*Ugh. And he found himself someone else to date.* The thought made Felicity's heart hurt.

"Just sayin'." Maia measured rice from a storage container and added it to the boiling water.

"Yeah, well, don't start reading too much into anything. He has a date tonight with Macks. I'd think if he was interested in me, he would ask me out. And not on a work date. Besides, I think he's taking her to the ball. So...there ya go."

"Then you go sit with Kevin at his table," Maia said. She used tongs to pick up the chicken breasts that were on a plate on the counter and place them into a skillet to sauté.

"Well, I did tell Kevin I'd be his date." Felicity watched her friend season the cooking poultry. "I'll have to work some that night, but I'm sure he's expecting me to sit with him when I can. But as far as Kevin goes, this is it, Maia. I'm not going to see him anymore. The only reason I said I'd be his date is so he'd buy the table and support the foundation. I feel kind of weird about that."

Maia shook her head. "If Kevin can use you for business, then there's no harm in you using him to get a hefty donation for the foundation. Or to get Austin's attention. It's good that you'll have a date. That way you won't have to sit there and watch him dance with that woman all night long."

"I'm not exactly attending the ball as a guest. I'll be busy." Her stomach rumbled. She put her hand on her middle, unsure if it was hunger or envy that he would be holding Macks on the dance floor. "That smells delicious. What are you making for dinner?"

"Chicken and rice. Want to stay and eat with me?"

Maia's cooking was always good and tonight Felicity needed company, so she wouldn't sit in her silent house and brood over Austin being with Macks at her art opening, wondering if they'd go out for drinks or dinner afterward. If he'd stay at her place…or bring her back to his.

"I'd love to," Felicity said. "I have a bottle of sauvignon blanc in the refrigerator. I'll go get it."

With the help of a good friend and a little liquid courage, she would make it through this night without being tempted to do a drive-by of the art show.

Felicity smiled to herself. Or she could forego the wine and take a little after-dinner drive to see what she could see.

After she'd added the date to Austin's calendar, she'd done a little research and discovered Macks owned the Chanson de Vache gallery, where the show would take place. It was located in the artsy Warehouse District. Pictures on the website showed that the front of the gallery was floor-to-ceiling glass. She'd get a glimpse of what was going on by simply driving by.

Back at Maia's house, she stowed the wine in the refrigerator. "Want to do something a little outrageous?"

Maia's eyes lit up. "Always. What do you have in mind?"

Fifteen minutes later, they were in Maia's car heading up Tchoupitoulas Street toward the gallery on Julia Street. Claiming she wasn't hungry yet, Maia had gladly put aside her chicken and rice dinner to join Felicity on the adventure.

The reception was from seven o'clock to nine. There was a little less than an hour left.

"I didn't realize it was so late," Felicity said as they turned onto Julia Street. "We may have missed him."

"Let's drive by and see," Maia said. "You know, Austin and I have never seen each other face-to-face. If you want, I could go in and scope out the scene for you, get a barometer reading of the situation."

"Oh, there it is," Felicity said as they pulled up to a stop sign at the corner. The car was directly in front of the gallery. There was no one behind them, so it gave them both a chance to look inside the windows. That's when Felicity saw him. Austin was holding a glass of wine, standing by himself frowning at what looked like a giant red papier-mâché dress that might have come from the closet of *Alice in Wonderland*'s Queen of Hearts. To the left, was a similar dress in black and white.

From the looks of it, Felicity just knew that this wasn't Austin's favorite type of gig. Yet, he was still there—

A car horn sounded behind them. Before Felicity could look away, Austin looked toward the street and their gazes locked.

\* \* \*

*Felicity?*

Austin blinked and the woman in the car was gone.

He gave his head a quick shake, blinked again. He was worse off than he thought if he was seeing her face when she wasn't even there. It was ridiculous.

He pulled out his phone to text her and ask her if she was anywhere in the Warehouse District vicinity, but even if she said yes, what then? He couldn't very well invite her to join him here at Macks's gallery. However, he could ask her if she was busy, if she could meet him for a drink.

Right.

With a glass of wine in hand, he glanced around the gallery, trying to find something to distract himself so that he didn't do something that he regretted. He took in the white walls that were dotted with framed art that was not part of this art opening. Beta Perez, the artist that Macks was featuring this evening, was the creator of gigantic paper dress sculptures. There were five of them perched on the gray slate floors. Each one nearly grazed the fifteen-foot ceilings. Though Austin had made his rounds through the gallery, looking at everything, even the paintings and etchings on the walls, he marveled again at the sheer scale of the dresses.

He didn't know anyone besides Macks and Beta, the artist, whom he'd met when Macks had introduced him after he'd arrived. Macks and Beta were both talking to people, as they should.

While sculptures weren't Austin's style, and he couldn't imagine where someone would put a piece of art that big, someone was bound to fall in love with them. Wouldn't they? Why else would Macks have offered Beta a showing? He hoped she sold everything they were showing tonight and others that were specially commissioned.

And dammit, he was still thinking about Felicity and how he could be in the middle of a crowd like this and she still felt like his safe place. What would be the harm in seeing if she wanted to meet for a drink?

He drained the rest of his wine, took his phone out of his pocket and started to compose a text to her when Macks walked up.

"I'm sorry I haven't been able to talk to you much tonight, but I am the host."

"No apology necessary, I understand. Duty calls and you seem to be very good at what you do."

She batted her eyelashes at him. He noticed they were unnaturally long and sweeping. Macks was a beautiful woman, but Felicity wore just enough makeup to look pretty and pulled together. Austin couldn't help but think about how he preferred Felicity's natural beauty to Macks's worldly glamour.

"Why, thank you, kind sir," Macks said.

"I'm almost ready to kick out the stragglers who are only here for the food and wine. After I lock up, we're moving this party to Masquerade so we can dance. I'm driving. You can ride with me. Just the two of us."

Something he was learning about Macks was that she did love to be in the driver's seat. For that matter, so did Felicity, but she had a way of making him feel as if he was along for the ride, whereas sometimes,

Macks made it feel as if she'd tied him to the back bumper and was dragging him.

"Where is Masquerade?" he asked.

"It's in Harrah's." Macks laughed. "Oh, dear, don't tell me you've never been dancing at Masquerade."

Austin chuckled. Okay, he wouldn't tell her. He also wouldn't mention that Harrah's was near the river, not too far from the French Quarter, at which she had turned up her nose the other night when he'd invited her out for a drink with his sister and Chaz.

In all fairness, Harrah's was a nice hotel where she wouldn't have to risk sullying her expensive heels as she might on Bourbon Street, but just as she hadn't been up for going out the other night, tonight he just wanted to go home.

"Austin Fortune, you do live a sheltered life." She reached out and toyed with his tie, keeping her gaze trained on it as she spoke. "That's one of the many reasons I will be so good for you." She kept her head angled down but glanced up at him through her eyelashes.

He wanted to take a step back, but she had him cornered. If he did, he'd bump one of the gigantic paper dresses.

"Sounds like fun, but I'm going to call it a night. I have a long day tomorrow."

Macks stuck out her bottom lip and she continued to tug on his tie. "I wish you would come." Her voice was uncharacteristically childlike. "All work and no play make Austin Fortune a very dull boy."

Austin snorted.

Macks flinched and dropped his tie. She took a step back. "What was that about?"

"I'm sorry," he said. "My sister said the exact thing a few days ago."

"Well, there seems to be a theme happening here. However, make no mistake, I'm definitely not your sister." Once again, she looked up at him through her lashes in that coquettish way that seemed to be her signature flirt move. "Come out and play with me tonight, Austin. I promise you'll have lots of fun."

His mind flashed back to Kelly and how she'd been so damn persistent, not taking no for an answer until she'd managed to get him exactly where she wanted him. He'd rather be a boring guy than get duped again.

*Fool me once, shame on Kelly and her lies and manipulation. Fool me twice, shame on me. Thanks, but no thanks, I'm not playing.*

While Macks came from a good family that had been in New Orleans even longer than his family had, there was something about her slightly overbearing ways that triggered his relationship post-traumatic stress. Macks was a sexy woman and he had a pretty good idea where they'd end up if he went dancing with her tonight.

While he found her attractive, there was no danger that he would fall for her. She simply wasn't his type. She was too pushy, too spoiled and high maintenance. A one-night stand would only complicate future business matters.

Since he had no intention of them being anything

more than friends, he needed to leave before things got more awkward.

"Good to see you tonight," he said. "But I really do need to leave now."

Macks leaned in for a good-night kiss, but Austin stepped to the left, taking care not to knock into the huge red dress sculpture. He set his wineglass on a tray the caterer had set against the wall. The two of them were not going anywhere. No sense in leading her on.

Macks seemed to understand that because she was suddenly all business.

"Thanks for coming tonight, Austin. Please let me know if I can help you or Fortune Investments with any art needs in the future."

After Austin stepped out into the balmy night, he pulled up Felicity's number and texted, Are you up for a drink?

Before he reached the car, she had replied, Sure.

## Chapter Nine

When Felicity walked into the Sazerac Bar in the Roosevelt Hotel, Austin was already waiting for her. When he saw her, he smiled and lifted a glass of amber-colored liquid in greeting. If he'd realized she was the woman in the car outside of Chanson de Vache gallery, he certainly didn't look irritated about it. If he was, surely, he wouldn't have invited her for a drink.

Their gazes were locked as she walked toward him, taking her time, happy that she'd put on a dress and let Maia mess with her hair, making it look stylishly un-coiffed in a way that Felicity would've never been able to accomplish if she'd been left to her own devices.

Of course, there was another matter that she couldn't overlook. Austin had gone to Macks's art show earlier that evening, but now he was sitting in the back corner of a cozy hotel bar waiting for her.

The thought was empowering.

When she reached the table, Austin stood.

"Thanks for coming out on such short notice," he said as he helped her settle herself on the plush chair that was next to his.

"Everything okay?" She held her breath, plunging into the question without second-guessing herself. If he had realized she'd been in the car and he had an issue or a question about it, it was best to get it out of the way straight away.

"Everything is fine." He knocked back the rest of his drink.

"How was the art show?"

He grimaced, shrugged. "It was great, if oversize paper dresses are your thing."

He motioned to the server and explained the show's concept to Felicity as he waited for the server to come over and take Felicity's drink order. She ordered a Sazerac, since the famous rye whiskey libation was the drink of the house as well as its namesake. Austin ordered another one, too.

"The art show sounds very *Alice in Wonderland*–esque."

Austin chuckled. "I definitely felt as if I'd drunk the shrinking potion and fallen down the rabbit hole, which, according to the artist's statement, is exactly what she intended, but I don't want to talk about that right now."

She loved the feel of his gaze on her. In a split second, she tamped down the temptation to ask him where Macks was and why he wasn't with her, but why invite the woman to wedge herself between them if she wasn't there?

Okay. If this was her chance, she was not going to blow it by talking about Macks or suddenly becoming awkward and difficult to talk to. The two of them had never had trouble making conversation. Why was her mind going blank now?

"This is a nice little spot." Even if she had to grab onto the obvious, it was better than talking about the weather. "You know, despite the number of times I've been to the Roosevelt Hotel on errands for the ball, I've never been in here."

"I'm glad we're here tonight," he said, and it made her heart thud a steady cadence that sounded an awful lot like *me too me too me too* in her own ears. "So, how are you?"

"I'm fine. Fine." She glanced around the room at the huge mirror behind the bar that reflected the moody lighting, the elegant woodwork and art deco murals. She felt suddenly shy, again at a loss for words. Not really knowing how to navigate the intimacy of the situation, should she dive into business discussion, which was comfortable territory? It wasn't very conducive for relaying the vibe that she was open for less business-y talk, or no talk at all…because she wouldn't mind one bit if he wanted to maybe, say…lean in and kiss her.

The thought made her breath hitch and Austin must've noticed because he squinted at her as if trying to assess if he should ask her what she was thinking. But he didn't. Instead, he surprised her with something totally unexpected.

"Good," he said. "And I'm about to make your night even better."

"Oh?" The word squeaked out. Because, again, she lost her breath at the thought of him leaning in and tasting her lips right here in front of everyone in the Sazerac Bar, in the Roosevelt Hotel, where next weekend they would host one of New Orleans's most exclusive charity balls.

Austin cleared his throat. "On my way over here, my father called. He wants to interview you about your ideas for advertising Fortune Investments."

"What? Are you serious?"

Austin smiled. "Believe me, I wouldn't kid about something like that. I think we need to celebrate."

He signaled to the server and ordered a bottle of Chandon Brut before Felicity could object. And she really didn't want to object because opportunities to sip bubbly with Austin didn't come along every night.

"Thanks, but aren't we a little premature celebrating at this point?" she said.

Austin smiled that smile that turned her inside out every single time. "I'm a firm believer that you need to celebrate every step along the way, no matter how small."

She laughed. "I like your style, Fortune."

He laughed, too, leaning on the arm of his chair. She mirrored him, angling toward him. When the laughter trailed off, their gazes snared, and they were looking at each other in a way that made Felicity's stomach do a double loop.

"What does this mean?" she asked, realizing too late how personal it sounded. "I mean, what will Miles expect in the interview?"

Austin sat back in his chair and seemed to seriously consider her question from the business angle, which left her with mixed emotions. "I can find out more, but from what I gather, he wants you to outline how advertising will benefit the company. You know Miles. He is driven by the bottom line. If you can show him in black and white how you, as director of advertising, will help Fortune Investments make money, he'll hire you in a heartbeat."

Felicity blinked. The only problem was she hadn't yet worked in advertising. Her experience was all academic. She stopped herself midthought. This was the opportunity of a lifetime—or at least for this moment in her lifetime. It wasn't the time to weigh herself down with negative thoughts. She had resources through her professors. She would ask them for help—

"When does Miles want to talk to me? I need time to put together a presentation."

"It won't be until after the gala. He knows you have enough on your plate with that, but, Felicity, he has also recognizes your hard work. He thinks you're a real asset to the company and he doesn't want to lose you. So, basically the position is yours. You just have to go in there and claim it."

Austin raised his lowball glass to her and smiled, but somehow the sentiment wasn't in his eyes.

"Are you okay with this?" she asked.

"Of course. I am behind you one hundred percent. I want what's best for you, even though we both know that the gain of the future Fortune Investments advertising department is my loss. I just have to rethink the way I was going to approach some things."

Felicity blinked at his choice of words. His last sentence came out as more of an afterthought. She wondered if he'd meant to say the words aloud. *Rethink his approach?* To what? Her heart did a quickstep as she mentally relived the moment they'd shared earlier. And the way he'd looked at her when she'd walked in. Or had she imagined it? Maybe the vibe she was sensing now was because a change for her would mean a big change for him, too.

She'd spoiled him. That was the part of her job she loved the most. Now that she thought about it, that little pang she was feeling when she should've been over-the-moon excited about the opportunity he'd just laid in her lap was the thought of someone else being that close to him. When she wouldn't be anymore. She and Austin were about as intimate as two people could be without being…intimate.

"If I do get the advertising position, you know I'll be there to help whomever you hire to be your new assistant."

At the thought, a pang pierced her. If she stayed at Fortune Investments, what would become of the two of them? Would they drift apart, or would they finally get the chance to explore this *thing* she felt pulsing between them? If they did get the chance, it wouldn't be anytime soon because she just couldn't see Miles smiling on her having a personal relationship with his son when Miles was taking the chance on her to break ground in a brand-new position.

"I know, but that's not what I…" He trailed off without completing his thought.

*What, Austin? Say it.* She had to bite the insides of her cheeks to keep from blurting it out. But why shouldn't she? He started it. He obviously had more to say. He'd called her to meet him tonight. He'd said he got the call from Miles as he was on his way here. That meant he'd wanted to meet for a drink before he'd had the news.

"What, Austin? Say it."

He opened his mouth. Shut it. She reached out and put her hand on his. He turned his hand over so that they were palm to palm. Then he shifted and laced his fingers through hers, taking possession of her hand. His thumb caressed small circles up her index finger in a way that told her more than anything he could've said. She melted on the inside and her lady parts sang an intimate version of the "Hallelujah" chorus because finally, *finally*, after all these years—

"Felicity. I want you—" He choked on the words and cleared his throat. "I want you to get this job."

*Oh.*

His thumb stopped the circles and she withdrew her hand, placing it in her lap as she comprehended what he was trying to say. But what could she say, besides—

"Thanks?" She shifted away from him and picked up her drink that was on the low cocktail table in front of them. She took a long pull, draining the glass. The dry, spicy shock of the rye helped her gather herself and regroup. She was just about to say she had to go when the server delivered the sparkling wine.

She considered bowing out and leaving him with the bottle that the woman had just opened with a flourish and a subtle *pop-pffft*. But she didn't want to go. It had been another herky-jerky night full of mixed signals and contradictions. So, what was new?

Actually, there was something new. Something had shifted between them. It was subtle, but it was something. Only right now, she didn't know what to do about it, other than get things back on track.

Austin handed her a flute of bubbly. "Here's to what comes next."

*Gaaa!* There it was again.

*What's next, Austin? A chance for us? Is there a chance for us?*

"Cheers." She touched her glass to his and sipped the effervescent liquid.

"Are your sister and her boyfriend still here?" Felicity knew they were was since Savannah had mentioned she was staying in New Orleans until after the ball, but the question was a sure path to get them back on solid ground. Solid ground that wasn't business.

"They are," Austin said. "But I don't know how long they'll stay."

"Why? What's going on?"

And just like that, the murky vibe that had clouded emotions moments ago had dissipated and they were back on track. Austin gave her the rundown on Gerald's wedding and the safety concerns caused by the other incidents. "Savannah and Chaz are hell-bent on attending even though my parents are against it. My sister has seized on the aspect that Gerald is family and family supports each other in good times and bad. My parents are of the mind that we just learned that Gerald is family. So, it's not worth the risk."

"So, you're related to *those* Fortunes?" Since he brought it up, Felicity figured there was no harm in asking.

Austin sipped his wine, looking thoughtful. "We are. My dad was raised by my grandmother. She was never very forthcoming about the identity of his father. Until he turned twenty-one and learned that his father was Julius Fortune. You know Miles. So, you can imagine how unimpressed he was about being related to the Fortunes. To prove it, he legally changed his name, but he didn't seek any connection to his father or his other relatives. It was a point of pride to prove that he could make it on his own. And he did.

"Miles built Fortune Investment from the ground up. He still doesn't want anything from anybody. I think even without the weird things that have been happening to his extended family, he'd still be reluctant about embracing them. That may be a large part of the reason he doesn't want to attend his half brother's wedding. The safety issue is a convenient excuse. I think he just doesn't want to get that close."

Austin shook his head and took another sip of his drink. Felicity didn't speak for fear of breaking the spell.

"You should be proud of yourself that Miles has embraced you the way he has," he went on. "You're the first person who isn't part of his immediate family that he's ever considered for upper management."

Austin gave her a pointed look that she couldn't quite read. Then he looked away, frowning at a spot somewhere in the distance. "My divorce left my dad pretty jaded."

"What do you mean, it made *him* jaded? It was your relationship."

Austin scoffed. "It's a long, sordid story. Are you sure you're up for this?"

"Of course I am." She held out her flute and Austin refilled it.

"When I was twenty-five, *Town & Country* magazine published an article about the south's most eligible bachelors," Austin said. "Yours truly was one of the men they spotlighted. I didn't know it at the time, but, Kelly, my ex-wife, saw the article and decided she was going to marry me. She didn't know me. We'd never met, but she knew I was her future husband."

"That's frightening."

"You haven't heard the half of it," he said. "Little did I know, but she started keeping tabs on me and followed me to New York City, where I was in town on business for a few weeks. During that time, she orchestrated a serendipitous meeting. She lied and passed herself off as an heiress who was spending time in the city before wintering in Europe, and she wooed me into believing it was love at first sight. I was such an idiot."

Austin blew out a breath, knocked back the rest of

his drink, topped off Felicity's glass and poured more for himself.

"After a two-week, whirlwind courtship we eloped without telling anyone." He shook his head at the memory. "She was *that* persuasive. And at the same time, she had this damsel-in-distress way about her that made me feel fiercely protective of her.

"When I brought my new wife home to New Orleans, my family was stunned and angry to learn that I had gotten married without telling anyone. My mom was crushed that her first child to the altar had eloped and cheated her out of her mother-of-the-groom honor.

"Miles was angry for a different reason. He did a background check and discovered that Kelly had misrepresented herself. She'd claimed to be an only child. She'd said her parents were dead and she'd inherited their wealth. When we decided to get married, she'd said that a traditional wedding would make her too sad since her father wouldn't be able to walk her down the aisle and her mother wouldn't be there to help her plan it. I believed her. In reality, she was divorced and financially strapped. She had maxed-out about a dozen credit cards trying to pull off her rich orphan charade. And the coup de grâce? Her parents weren't dead. They were in jail—convicted con artists."

Felicity's jaw fell open. She couldn't help it.

"Wait, there's more. She promised me that she was nothing like her family. She begged and pleaded for me to believe her. She said she couldn't tell me the truth because she was afraid that I wouldn't give her a chance, much less be able to love her, because of her family's wrongdoings. She said that my family's anger was case in point. She swore she loved me with all her heart and wanted our marriage more than anything in the world.

"Miles cut me off financially. I realized that would be the true test as to whether she wanted me or my family's money. And I wanted to prove my parents wrong. I wanted to believe Kelly and show them that we could make the marriage work. Plus, I was really pissed off at my father for taking it upon himself to dig into Kelly's background.

"So, to make a long story short, we managed to hold the marriage together for two years before other parts of Kelly's past began to catch up with her. I learned that I wasn't her first mark when a man that she'd stolen money from turned up, threatening to press charges and expose her. Miles bailed her out, for fear of what the scandal would do to our family and the business. No one wants to work with an investment company that has ties to swindlers, especially when they're trusting you with their money. But I had to pay back my father the money he'd spent to get the guy off our backs. Things went from tight to lean.

"Kelly grew restless. A few months later, I discovered she was having an affair and divorced her. After that, I learned that being married to my job was a whole hell of a lot safer than investing in a relationship."

It was a lot to digest. She knew he was divorced and judging by the way no one ever talked about it, she figured it had been a very unhappy marriage, but she never dreamed he'd been through something so horrific.

"I'm sorry that happened to you. Kelly really did a number on you, didn't she?"

"Yeah, I was pretty stupid to fall right into her trap."

"You know it's not your fault, Austin. She's the one who's to blame. You cannot blame yourself or let her make you jaded about love."

He shrugged. "Love? I don't believe in love. I don't think there's such a thing."

"How can you not, Austin? I'm one hundred percent sure love exists."

"But?" he countered.

"But what?" she asked.

"I heard an implied *but* at the end of your declaration."

"No, you didn't."

*Oh, my God.* He could read her like a book. Or read her thoughts, which was an even scarier prospect.

*Austin, if you can read my thoughts, it's okay for you to kiss me. Right here. Right now. Just do it.*

She discreetly moistened her lips, just in case. But he didn't lean in.

"It's okay," he said. "You don't have to tell me. I know how hard it is to talk about things like that. You're the first person outside of my family that I've told the full story of what happened with Kelly."

He'd trusted her with something so intimate, which made it even more crucial to not ruin his trust by doing something stupid like overstepping boundaries.

"I know love exists because I feel it—*err*—I've felt it. But I believe it never lasts. Once those feelings are pulled forth from behind the veil, it's as if there's a countdown to the end." She pointed to the bottle of Chandon that the server had left in the standing silver ice bucket.

"It's like that sparkling wine. Once you pop the cork, it's a countdown to when the bubbles go flat."

"Unless you drink the wine before it has a chance to lose all of its fizz."

Felicity arched a brow. "Oh, so you're admitting there is fizz."

"I was speaking hypothetically."

She smiled. "Sure you were. I think you're still letting Kelly hold a lot of power over you if you've let her rob you of your ability to ever love again."

*Let me love you, Austin. Let me show what real love is. I would never hurt you.*

It was on the tip of her alcohol-loosened tongue. But she closed her mouth, catching her lips between her teeth for extra assurance. She may have already revealed too much of herself without even saying how she felt.

Her heart hitched. Maybe their clock had already started—even before their love story had begun.

"If love does exist, but it doesn't last, then what's the point? Why subject yourself?"

"I ask myself that question every day."

His eyes widened.

*Oh, schizer.* She wanted to reel back the words, but it was too late.

"You do?"

"Hypothetically speaking," she said.

"Okay, but what made you feel this way? Did someone break your heart?"

She bowed her head for a moment and let the curtain of her hair hide her face while she gathered her thoughts.

"The other day when we were talking about my graduation," she said, looking up at him, "you asked me if my dad was coming to the ceremony."

Austin nodded.

"He's not, because my parents don't get along. They had a very bitter divorce when I was thirteen. Even all these years later, my mom just can't bring herself to be around him. The two of them had such a passionate relationship. When things were good, I remember it being so good. There was this time right before I turned ten that things were so good. It felt like it was the three of us against the world and nothing could touch us. It was such a happy moment in my life, I didn't realize that the clock was ticking down. When things started to fall apart, it got so ugly.

"My mom never remarried. She used to always say it was because anything that good, anything with that much power over you, can't last. In the end, it will hurt ten times more than the good it once brought. I'm not going to lie—I know I let their experience affect my feelings. I mean, a father is the first guy a little girl loves. He's supposed to be the one man who will always love you and protect you, and if he breaks your heart, how can you believe anything like love will ever last?"

The next morning as Austin walked to work, he replayed last night's events over in his mind. He hadn't been drunk, but he hadn't exactly been sober either. He had been nicely relaxed, and his tongue had been loose enough that he had confessed his life story to Felicity.

She'd been equally forthcoming in giving him a glimpse into her past, a peek at what had shaped her to be the woman he knew and cared for so damn much it was almost a physical ache.

How was it that they had worked together so long and so closely and he'd never known that about her? The most sobering part about it was, this morning, in the light of day, he didn't regret baring his soul. Or at least that's what he was telling himself. Because there was no taking it back. What was done was done. He only hoped he hadn't overwhelmed her.

If it took opening up to her to make her open up to him, it was well worth the risk. He was finding it more and more difficult to deny the feelings that had surfaced since he'd been faced with the possibility of her walking out of his life forever.

If it hadn't been for Miles's ill-timed call about a meeting today, last night may have ended in a very different way. He'd wanted her, and he'd finally decided it was time to stop fighting it. His father's call, which came just as they were at the end of the wine, had been an intervention that might have saved him from making a colossal mistake.

Felicity's promotion was important. Austin knew he needed to put her future over these confusing feelings that were clouding his judgment. She would probably get the advertising job, but Miles would probably end up firing them both if they broke the cardinal rule of not fraternizing. Blood be damned, Miles would have no compunction about sacking one of his own children if they didn't follow the rules.

Reliving the story about what happened with Kelly was a good reminder of that. Miles had cut him off in heartbeat and it had taken Austin a solid five years to work himself back into his father's good graces. He couldn't jeopardize that for these strange feelings that had suddenly materialized.

He hadn't been in his right mind last night. Actually thinking he'd seen Felicity in a car parked outside the gallery. In retrospect, the woman in the car hadn't looked anything like her. The woman's eyes had been large and haunted, not at all like Felicity's. While she wasn't the blind eternal optimist, she had a way of holding herself that was so steadfast. Even in his darkest times, even being near her gave Austin hope. But if he knew what was best for everyone, he needed to keep a professional distance between Felicity and himself. At least until he could sort out these feelings and get them under control.

As Austin exited the elevator and navigated the long corridor to their little corner of the Fortune Investments world, he contemplated whether he should invite Macks to the ball. Felicity would be there as Kevin's date. The thought sent pinpricks of irritation coursing through him. Even though she'd said she wasn't interested in Kevin and was only going to the gala with him because that had been a stipulation of his donation. Austin had driven home the point that she didn't have to do that, but she had still insisted on going with him. Maybe that meant she wanted to?

Even if it would be difficult to watch her with the guy, he wasn't going to invite Macks. He didn't want to make her think he was interested in her in any way that wasn't platonic. Maybe seeing Kevin with Felicity, as painful as it would be, was exactly what he needed to get over her and on with his life. As he rounded the corner, he heard her on the phone. She was using her all-business voice. He hoped she wasn't upset about last night.

"I'm sorry, Ms. Cole, I can't give you Mr. Fortune's personal cell number. I'm happy to take yours and give it to him."

Felicity thought Austin had called Macks from his personal phone. He must've used his work cell phone. He had two, and he guarded his personal line jealously.

"Felicity, isn't it?" Macks asked.

"Yes."

"Felicity, I thought we were friends. Friends take care of friends."

Good grief, the woman was persistent. She was probably the type who wasn't used to people telling her no.

"I'm sure they do. But I still can't give you Mr. Fortune's personal number."

Macks growled. She actually growled. Low and guttural. "When will he be in?"

"I don't know."

"You don't know?" Now she'd switched into superiority mode. Her words were clipped and crisp. So much for being friends. "Aren't you the one who keeps his calendar? Isn't it your job to know?"

Felicity looked up and saw Austin standing there. She made a face and pointed to the phone. He mouthed, *Who is that?*

On her notepad, she wrote, *Macks Cole. Shall I tell her you're in?*

He shook his head and waved her off. Then he took the pen from her hand. His hand brushed hers and she flashed back to last night when he'd held her hand.

He wrote on her notepad, *Coffee before Macks. I'll call her back.* The way he smiled at her put her completely at ease. He wasn't acting differently toward her after sharing such a big part of himself with her last night. In fact, it felt as if the two of them shared a secret—a few secrets, actually. The intimacies they'd shared last night and the fact that Macks wanted to talk to him, but he didn't seem very eager.

"I'll have Mr. Fortune call you at his earliest convenience," Felicity said into the phone.

Austin reached over her and pushed the speaker phone button in time to hear Macks say, "I certainly hope you do, because after I talk to Austin and tell him how unaccommodating you were, it could mean your job."

Their gazes locked. Austin frowned, and Felicity simply raised her brows at him.

"I will relay your message, Ms. Cole. Have a nice day."

Felicity heard a click and the line went dead.

"Good morning," she said.

Austin shook his head. "What a nightmare way for you to start the day. I'm sorry. You don't have to put up with that."

Felicity shrugged. "I couldn't very well hang up on her."

"Oh, I don't know. I hear the phone lines in this office can be temperamental. Sometimes people get disconnected. Especially when they act like jackasses. What set her off?"

"She wanted me to give her your personal cell phone number. I figured if you hadn't already given it to her, you might not want her to have it."

"Good call," Austin said. "I don't want her to have it, especially after hearing that much of the conversation. Forget her."

There had never been two words that made Felicity happier. "Aren't you taking her to the gala?"

Austin grimaced. "No. I never got around to asking her." He looked at her in a way that made Felicity's pulse kick up. "Now I'm glad I didn't. But speaking of the gala, do you have moment?"

"Of course."

"Good. Grab your coffee and come into my office. Our conversation last night made me realize something."

In the back of Felicity's mind, a wild daydream played out. Austin was asking her to be his date to the ball. But before she could close the distance between her desk and his office, she had grounded herself with the absurdity of the thought and reminded herself that it was a good thing that he couldn't read her thoughts.

"Talking about my family's wedding dilemma last night made me realize that our gala might be at risk, too. I think we need to hire security to make sure Charlotte Prendergast Robinson doesn't try to pull anything. She's been too quiet for too long. I don't know if it's because she's lying low, knowing she's being watched… After all, Savannah says the authorities are on to her. Then again, it's possible that they have the wrong person and Charlotte isn't the perpetrator. What if someone else has been targeting the Fortunes all this time and the authorities have been after the wrong person? It's all a big question mark. I know it's a lot to ask this close to the event, but I think we need to make sure we have a strong but discreet security presence at the charity ball. Because the reality is at a gathering like this, we could be in serious trouble."

## Chapter Ten

Felicity did a twirl in front of the mirror in her suite at the Roosevelt. The fitted red ball gown hugged her curves like it was made for her. The strapless corset top nipped in her waist, making it look tiny, before it flared into a chiffon, A-line skirt that made her feel like a princess.

Maia had come by and had done her makeup and hair, leaving it to fall in soft curls around her shoulders.

Felicity did one more twirl, wistfully taking it all in, before she grabbed her clutch purse that contained her hotel room key, lipstick and compact for touch-up. There wouldn't be time to run up to the room once the ball got started. But she could if she needed to. That's part of the reason why the suite was such a nice gift from Austin.

Austin had surprised her with the key card yesterday. He'd arranged for early check-in. She'd arrived with her dress, shoes and accessories for the gala and a suitcase for the night. That had made it possible for her to spend the morning supervising the transformation of the ballroom from ordinary beautiful to gala extraordinary. Then she'd taken the elevator back up to her room, showered and let Maia help her get ready for the big event.

The other part of why it was so wonderful was tonight, when all was said and done, all she had to do was ride the elevator back to the tenth floor and she was home for the night. She'd worked hard this week, verifying last-minute details and lining up the security that would unobtrusively blend into the background. It had been a good call on Austin's part. Due to all the disturbances that had been swirling around the Fortunes, both near and far, it was better to be safe than sorry. However, it had taken some doing on her part to find the security personnel at this late date. She'd been forced to jump through several hoops to pull it off, but she had.

As she walked into the ballroom, she looked around at the gold-and-white wonderland. Stunning arrangements of white flowers displayed in towering gold vases offset by pearlescent linens and gold Chiavari chairs. Flickering white-and-gold candles rested atop mirrored bases that reflected the light. Elegant china, crystal and fine flatware set the stage for the sumptuous meal to come, which was detailed on the engraved gold-and-white menu cards placed atop the plates. The silent auction items were lined up on tables around the perimeter of the room. The band was doing a final sound check.

Felicity glanced at her phone, checking the time and making sure there were no SOS calls from the league of foundation volunteers who had agreed to help out tonight. There were still fifteen minutes until the doors would open and the guests would spill in. Before she'd let herself into the ballroom, she'd checked on the early volunteers who were seated at tables in the atrium near the ballroom, ready to check in the guests as they arrived.

Everything was in place and it all looked absolutely perfect. She took a minute to close her eyes, take a deep breath and savor the calm before the party started. When she opened her eyes, Austin was walking toward her, looking stunning in his Armani tux. She knew it was Armani, because she'd gone with him to render an opinion when he'd purchased it. Like something out of a dream, he floated toward her, smiling. The sight of him made her lips curve upward, too.

"Would it violate a human resources rule or make you feel uncomfortable if I said you look absolutely gorgeous tonight?"

"Not at all, because so do you," she returned, basking in the glow of his compliment and feeling just this side of giddy because of how all her hard work had come together. "You clean up well, Fortune."

Actually, he wore a suit to work every day and looked gorgeous. But this tux was above and beyond.

"Yeah, well, I try," he said. "I met with the security

team. I have all but four stationed by the check-in tables. I have one in the lobby, one at valet and two are in this room." Austin pointed to two well-built men dressed in tuxedos, one stationed at each door. Felicity had thought they were part of the waitstaff.

"They look great. They'll blend right in."

"They all have a photo of Charlotte and if they notice anything suspicious, I've instructed them to call the police right away."

"Looks like we're covered," Felicity said. She opened her handbag and pulled out a piece of paper with the evening's schedule, which she went over with Austin one more time. It was nice to stand so close to him. She could smell his shampoo and aftershave. The combination that smelled like cedar, coffee and leather was so uniquely him, it made her long to lean in closer and breathe in deeper. But, Lisa, their contact from the hotel, approached with a walkie-talkie and the list detailing the order of events.

Lisa had agreed to work with Felicity to help ensure that the program stayed on track. Austin would be the emcee for the evening, but Felicity would be close by to cue him if he needed to know what came next.

Felicity started to review a few points. "After the doors open, we'll give people about an hour to get drinks and bid on the items in the silent auction—"

Her phone buzzed. It was a text from Kevin telling her he was at the hotel.

Come have a drink with me. I want to introduce you to my entourage.

Quickly Felicity texted back. Sorry, going over the final details of the gala. See you when the doors open.

Let me in now. I'll bring you a drink.

She didn't answer because she knew he would continue to argue the point. He and his *entourage*—who even said something like that?—would just have to entertain themselves.

When the doors opened, Kevin and his buddies—five guys and a woman—found her straight away. Unfortunately, Felicity was in the middle of trying to locate a missing basketball that had been signed by the New Orleans Pelicans. It had been there before the doors opened because she and Lisa had double-checked all the silent auction items.

Kevin made quick introductions and then she had to scurry off to locate the missing ball, which, it turned out had rolled off its stand and under the table skirt.

The next time Kevin found her, she was with Austin in one of the hallways off the ballroom that led to the kitchen, coaching him on his welcome remarks.

"Sorry to interrupt." Kevin seemed a little miffed and looked at them like he'd stumbled upon a secret liaison. "Your dinner is still on the table. The servers keep trying to take it away. Do you want it?"

"Kevin, I'm so sorry," she said. "After the opening remarks and the first dance, things should slow down a little. Thanks for bearing with me until then."

He grunted something she didn't quite catch and then disappeared out the way he'd come.

Austin's welcome speech went off perfectly. The only small hitch to the program came right before he was supposed to take the dance floor with his sister, when Savannah's shoe broke. The first dance was traditionally danced by a couple of the Fortunes and it was meant to get the party started. This year, the honor was Austin and Savannah's.

"Felicity, I can't go out there in bare feet. I'll step on my dress." Savannah held up a pair of five-inch heels.

"Do you want to wear my shoes?" Felicity offered, noticing too late how tiny Savannah's feet were compared to Felicity's own size nines.

"Thanks for offering, but I don't think that will work," she said as the band played another riff of the song that preceded the first dance. Lisa had scurried over to let the bandleader know what was holding up the show and now, the singer was trying to stretch out the song until they were ready.

"Will you dance with Austin, Felicity?" Savannah suggested.

Felicity glanced around the room looking for Belle or Georgia or even Sarah, but they all seemed to be well hidden. She really didn't have a choice.

There was something in Savannah's smile that hinted that her shoe malfunction might not have been an accident. And then it hit Felicity—she would get to dance with Austin.

"Are you okay with this?" she asked him.

"Sure," he returned, his expression unreadable.

Savannah signaled to Lisa and pointed to Felicity. Lisa seemed to get the message because she told the bandleader and he announced, "Mr. Austin Fortune, dancing with Miss Felicity Schafer."

When Austin took her into his arms, she felt like she'd finally found her home. They swayed together, his hand on the small of her back, their bodies moving in time to the music. For a few short minutes the rest of the world melted away and it was just her in the arms of the man she loved.

All too soon, the music changed from the slow, romantic song to something more upbeat. The singer was inviting the rest of the guests to join them on the dance floor, and Felicity felt a hand on her shoulder.

She looked up to see Kevin ask Austin, "May I cut in, please?"

"Sure," Austin said. "You kids have fun."

*No! Don't go.*

But he did. He walked off as Kevin tried to pull her into slow dance form despite the up-tempo song. Felicity resisted by taking her hand and spinning herself out in a modified swing dancing move. At the end of the song, which seemed to go on forever, she told him she was thirsty and needed something to drink. Like a good date, Kevin was off to the bar to get her something.

By the time he returned, about ten minutes later, it was time for Felicity to help facilitate the silent auction results. She thanked him for the drink and explained what she needed to do. But before she could get away, he asked, "How long do you think you'll be? My friends left after dinner. They had another party."

Felicity felt a little sorry for him for spending all that money only to share his table with people who would ditch him? And she knew she was being a lousy date, but she had warned him that she had to work the event.

"Why don't you ask someone to dance?" Felicity suggested. "I'm sure there are plenty of women who would love to." Even though most of the women were there with dates. Still, she had no choice but to excuse herself and get to work, leaving Kevin with a glass of scotch and a long face.

As Austin passed by Kevin Clooney's table, Kevin stood and blocked his way.

"If I didn't know better," Kevin slurred, "I'd think you were purposely trying to keep Felicity and me apart tonight. What the hell, Fortune? What's your problem?"

Clooney had a glass of what looked like scotch, straight up, in his hand. Judging by the way he was slurring his words, it wasn't his first drink of the evening. Probably not his third either. He had pulled his tie loose and unbuttoned the first button at the collar. Austin glanced around for one of the security personnel they'd hired, but they were surveilling the entrances and exits.

"I don't have a problem, Clooney," Austin said. "But I think you've had a little too much to drink. You either need to settle down or I'll call you a car and get someone to help you down to the lobby."

"I don't need your help, Fortune." As a waiter walked by, Clooney held up his half-full glass and motioned for a refill. In the process, some of the amber liquid sloshed over the side. As Clooney transferred his glass to his other hand and clumsily wiped the liquor on the leg of his tuxedo pants, Austin caught the waiter's eye and gave a subtle shake of the head. He mouthed the word *water*. The waiter nodded and mouthed back, *Security?* Austin gave a subtle nod.

"Look, I get it," said Kevin. "You don't like me. Honestly, I don't like you either, but business is business and I need to get someone to bankroll my restaurant. But you—" He jabbed his index finger in the middle of Austin's chest.

Austin caught his hand and held it in midair before dropping it with a firm flick of his wrist. The movement caused the guy to stagger back a few steps.

He really wanted to walk away, but he needed to stay until security arrived and stopped Kevin from making an even bigger scene.

"Yeah, you. You're just a big, fat waste of my time," Kevin slurred. "But I guess that doesn't matter to you, does it? You're a Fortune. You don't care about the little people. Except for Felicity. I think you like her. And the real kicker is I think she likes you, too. But the only reason a chick like her would be interested in a loser like you is because of your money."

That was rich, coming from a guy who'd spent twenty-five hundred dollars on a table and the so-called friends he'd invited to share it with him had apparently deserted him. Austin almost felt sorry for the guy. But it was kind of difficult to muster the empathy between the insults the guy was hurling at him. The only reason Austin hadn't walked away was because as host, it was his responsibility to make sure the guy didn't provoke someone else.

"You're not the only game in town, Fortune." He bellowed the words and people were starting to stare. "I can walk out of here and have the money I need by the end of the month."

"There's the door," Austin said, gesturing with a wide sweep. "No one is stopping you. In fact, it would probably be a good idea if you left. Let me call you a car. You're in no shape to drive."

"I can drive if I want to," Kevin slurred and slurped what was left of his drink.

"Good luck getting your keys from the valet."

Kevin smirked. "This isn't even about business, is it? It's about Felicity. You take and take and take from the little guy. You probably don't even want her, but you can't stand to see her with someone like me. Yeah, her and me, we're just disposable goods to guys like you."

Austin's blood started to boil at Clooney's mention of Felicity. But he wasn't going to let himself be baited by a drunk who would probably regret his foul attack as much as he regretted the hangover that was sure to hammer his thick head tomorrow morning.

"You might have all the money in the world, but you didn't have to work for one cent of it. I don't think you even know what it's like to work hard to get a woman like Felicity."

Now he wasn't even making sense.

"You kept her busy all night to keep her away from me. Didn't you?"

"That's her job. That's what I pay her to do."

"You get her to do all the hard work, so you can sit on your candy ass because you've never had to work hard for anything in your life. You don't have the character. You ain't got nothin', Fortune."

Where the hell was security? If Clooney got any more agitated, Austin was prepared to walk him outside himself. But he hated to create any more of a spectacle than had already been made.

"She deserves someone a whole hell of a lot better than you." Clooney shoved Austin's shoulder, but Clooney was the one who staggered backward. In the process, his arm knocked over a glass of champagne that was still sitting on Kevin's empty table.

Finally, security arrived. The guy put a hand on Kevin's shoulder. "Come on, buddy. I'm going to help you get home."

As security walked Clooney toward the door, Kevin said a few choice words as he tried to pull out of the guard's grasp. "I can find my own way out."

Then Felicity walked into his path. "Fortune wants you," he told her. "I think you want him, too." He twisted around, and his legs got tangled up as the security guard continued his forward motion. He would've fallen, if not for the guard holding him upright. Sadly, it didn't silence him. "Go for it. You two deserve each other."

With a horrified expression on her face, Felicity joined Austin and they watched Clooney stagger out the door.

"What in the world was that about?" she said.

"Your date had a little too much to drink. He's kind of an angry drunk."

"Well, there goes my ride," she joked. "It's a good thing I'm staying here at the hotel and don't need a driver."

"I'll walk you home," Austin said. "It's probably my fault he got so drunk. He said I worked you too hard tonight and kept you from him. Did I?"

Felicity laughed. "Are you kidding? He knew I had to work tonight. It didn't help matters when he got a little handsy out there on the dance floor."

"It's a good thing I didn't see that," Austin said. "I would've thrown him out a long time ago."

It was later than he realized, and soon the band announced their last number, a soulful rendition of *Can't Help Falling in Love*.

"Dance with me," Austin said.

He offered his hand. She took it, and he pulled her into his arms. They swayed together to the music. When they'd danced earlier, it had been such a surprise, what with Savannah's sudden shoe malfunction. Austin chuckled to himself.

"What is it?" Felicity asked, her words hot in his ear.

"I was just thinking about the timing of my sister's broken shoe earlier this evening."

"Yes, that was unfortunate, wasn't it? Or fortunate, actually. Yes, I think it was fortunate." She rested her head on his shoulder, nestling into him.

He pulled her closer, marveling at how good she felt, at the way his hand felt on the small of her back, at how she fit so perfectly against him, her curves magically tucking into the dips in his body. Her hair smelled of flowers and sunshine and everything that was good and right in the world. He could get used to this. God, he wanted to get used to this and from the way she was leaning into him he got the feeling Felicity could, too.

## Chapter Eleven

After the ballroom emptied out, Austin and Felicity returned to the Sazerac Bar in the hotel. They had an hour before the place closed and both of them were too wound up to call it a night. They decided to have a casual debriefing over a bottle of well-deserved champagne since they didn't have to drive. As Austin said, they'd earned it after the event being a smashing success.

"This is the second week in a row that we're sipping champagne in the Sazerac," Felicity said. "Is this a new thing? Because, I could get used to it."

They clinked glasses. "All in all, I'd say the gala went off without a hitch," Austin said.

Felicity shrugged. "Except for the missing basketball and Kevin's drunken performance."

She started to add Savannah's broken shoe, but that hadn't been a hardship. Felicity noticed later that Savannah had been wearing a pair of shoes. Felicity didn't know whether she was able to fix hers or she had a spare pair up in her hotel room, but it didn't matter. If Savannah had orchestrated the shoe malfunction, she wanted to hug her. If she did, did it mean that she was quietly advocating for Felicity and Austin to be together? At least that was one Fortune in her corner.

"But the gala was sold out, thanks to Kevin grabbing the last available table," Austin offered. "And Charlotte was a no-show."

*And I got to dance with you, feel what it's like to be in your arms.* "That is true. We found the basketball and security discreetly handled Kevin. So, for all the important reasons, it was a pretty darn successful gala."

The bar was empty, except for the two of them and another couple, who looked so wrapped up in each other that they seemed oblivious to Austin and Felicity's presence. So, essentially, they were alone. The place felt like a cozy cocoon. Kevin, Macks, Charlotte and other inconveniences of the outside world seemed far away.

"Did you always want to go into advertising?" Austin asked as he refilled her glass.

"No, getting an undergrad degree in advertising and an MBA seemed like the most practical degrees for me. The most marketable."

"What would you have studied if practicality didn't matter?"

"Something that had to do with flowers."

"What? Like being a florist?"

Felicity laughed. "I've never heard of a florist degree. I think that's mostly on-the-job training."

Austin smiled. "Of course. I'll blame it on mental exhaustion and champagne. So, what would you have studied?"

"Something really nerdy like botany."

His brows lifted. "Really?"

"I wanted to be a botanist. I love flowers—especially roses. I wanted to experiment with creating new rose species."

"You seem to know a lot about roses already. Could you still do it as a hobby?"

Felicity scoffed. "Yeah, in all my spare time."

"You have to make time for the things you love," Austin said.

"This coming from the man who proudly proclaims he's married to his job."

"Touché."

Felicity shrugged. "You're right, though. Someday I'm going to get that greenhouse for my backyard. Then I'll do it. I'm weird like that. I don't want a fancy car, expensive shoes or a designer purse. I want a greenhouse."

"I don't think it's weird at all. It's kind of refreshing, actually."

Felicity wondered if he was thinking of Macks.

"Did you ever call Macks Cole back? We've been so busy with the gala that I didn't have a chance to ask you."

"I did."

Of course, if Macks hadn't talked to Austin, no doubt, she would've kept hounding Felicity until she did. But Felicity wanted to hear it from Austin.

"Did you give her your personal cell phone number like she wanted?"

"I did not."

"Why not?"

Austin smiled, and his right brow shot up, a look that Felicity could've inferred as *none of your business* or that Austin just didn't want to talk about it. But she wanted to know.

"I know it's none of my business, but I'll play the mental exhaustion and champagne card, too, and ask you anyway. I'll blame it on that and double down. Why not, Austin?"

"Because I didn't want to."

*Ugh, how did that go over?* Macks didn't like the word *no*.

"Good to know," Felicity said. "So, I guess that means you're not dating her anymore."

She'd already pushed this far, why stop now?

"I never was dating her. But while we're on the subject of dating, are you still seeing Kevin?"

"I'm not."

Austin's smile smoldered. "Very good to know."

After the champagne was finished and Austin had paid the bill, he offered to walk Felicity to her room. As fate—or booking a block of rooms would have it—both of their rooms were on the hotel's tenth floor, but hers was farther down the hall than his. Still, it didn't seem right to say good-night and let her walk the rest of the way alone.

So, they walked past his.

"This is me," she said and stopped in front of her door. "Thanks for the champagne." She pulled her card key out of her purse, but instead of opening the door, she leaned against it, gazing up at him.

She looked so damn gorgeous and her lips were so inviting. He wanted to lean in and kiss her, so they wouldn't have to talk anymore. He wanted to lose himself in the taste of her, bury his face in her silky, long hair and stay there until he forgot about the very real fact that she was leaving him, one way or another.

"What are we going to do next year without you to organize the gala?" he asked, because it was a legit question and because even though talking was the last thing he wanted to do right now, it was his last option and he was grasping at straws since he wasn't ready to say good-night. He was testing the waters to see if she wanted to call it a night. It was two o'clock in the morning. It was too late to suggest they go out somewhere else, and even though propriety wouldn't allow him to ask her into his suite for another drink, he was still stalling for time.

"No matter where I end up, your new assistant can always call me with any questions, and I've kept good notes over the years."

He rested his shoulder on the wall so that they were both leaning toward each other. "Just stay," he said. "Don't leave me. I know that's not fair, but—"

"I don't want to leave you. I may not work for you much longer, but if I can help it, I won't leave you."

He reached out and touched a strand of her hair, needing to know if it was as soft as it looked. It was. He twirled it around his finger.

Then the next thing he knew, her lips were brushing his. It was a feather-soft kiss. One that could've stopped there, if she'd wanted it to, if she'd turned around and let herself into her room.

But she didn't.

He rested his forehead on hers. Her lips were a fraction of an inch from his. "Felicity, I don't want you to regret this. I don't want you to think I took advantage of you—"

"I know exactly what I'm doing, exactly what we're about to do. I've wanted this for so long. I think you want me, too, Austin. Don't you?"

*If you only knew.*

She leaned in and those lips were teasing his neck, her hot, delicious breath was in his ear.

"Austin, I don't mind if you kiss me. I want you to kiss me and we don't have to stop there."

Every inch of his body responded as his arms fell around her waist and he pulled her into his body. She slid her hands down to his butt, closing the distance so that his body was perfectly aligned with hers.

He didn't give her the chance to say anything else. Their lips found each other, and he showed her exactly how much he wanted her. As her mouth opened under his, passion consumed him. That moment, if he'd had the key to her room, he would've opened the door and walked her backward right into the bedroom and made love to her. Instead, he deepened the kiss and pulled her even tighter against him.

He wasn't sure how long they stayed like that, but when they came up for air, Felicity looked dazed. Her hand flew up to her kiss-swollen lips.

That's when Austin realized someone was walking toward them. He turned and saw his father letting himself into one of the hotel rooms four doors down.

Felicity flinched away.

"Austin. Felicity."

"Dad."

Miles pinned them with a steely glare. His mouth was drawn into a tight, thin line. "It was a nice party. Let's…uh…talk about everything first thing Monday morning. My office."

The moment Felicity disappeared inside her hotel room, Austin's cell phone rang. He muted the volume, so it wouldn't disturb the other guests as he made his way down the hallway to his own room.

He let himself inside his room and answered. "Hello."

"You are damn lucky you took my call." Miles sounded as if he was spitting fire. Austin almost hung up on him.

"Yeah? And what if I hadn't? What would you have done?"

Miles didn't answer his question. Instead, he jumped right into the tirade that Austin knew was coming.

"What the hell is wrong with you, Austin? Fooling around with your personal assistant? Are you trying to get Fortune Investments slapped with a sexual harassment lawsuit? How stupid can you be?"

"It's not like that, Dad." Austin flung his tux jacket onto a chair and toed out of his patent leather loafers.

"Yeah, well, I have eyes. I know what I saw. I know exactly what was going on. So does everyone else who saw you dancing with her at the gala tonight. You just provided all the corroborating witnesses she will need when she gets pissed off at you and decides to sue our asses."

"All we did was dance." It was taking every ounce of strength Austin possessed to keep his voice low and level. The soft champagne buzz had evaporated. In its place, the start of a headache was beginning to pound. Austin scrubbed his free hand over his eyes and then raked his fingers through his hair.

"It didn't look like you were dancing in the hallway. Or maybe you were saving the dance for after you got inside the room."

"Go to hell, Miles. What we were doing is none of your business. I'm not sixteen years old. What makes you think you have the right to tell me how to live my life?"

"I don't care how old you are. When you work for me, I have the final say on things that will affect my business. Your fooling around with your assistant could come back to bite me in the ass."

"She's not going to be my assistant for much longer. I have feelings for her. Besides, I know Felicity. I've known her for almost five years. She's not like that. She wouldn't turn around and try to take us for a ride."

"That's what you said about Kelly and look at how things ended up. Look what it cost us. I had to bail out your ass."

"Really? Are you really going to keep bringing that up? Because if you are, I'm going to hang up on you right now. I paid you back every penny of what I owed you. So, I made a mistake with her. Felicity is not Kelly. I am not going to stand here at nearly three o'clock in the morning trying to justify my feelings. You do not get to dictate who I see."

"I do if the two of you work for Fortune Investments. You are not above the rules, Austin. And the rules state that there is no fraternizing. Especially when it comes to an executive fooling around with a subordinate."

Austin started to object, but Miles cut him off.

"I was seriously considering promoting her. But I think you just killed that for her. Monday morning, you need to accept her notice and then keep your distance from her."

"That's not fair, Dad. Felicity has worked hard for us and deserves to be recognized for her hard work. You're an idiot if you let her go."

*And so am I.*

"I don't know—" Miles started to say.

"Well, you'd better think about it, because if you deny her this promotion based on what you saw tonight, then you're giving her every reason to sue your ass."

"I guess that means you have some decisions to make, doesn't it?" Miles said. "You have to choose, Austin. Do you want her to have the promotion? Or do you want to have your little fling? Because if you insist on fooling around with her, as far as I'm concerned, the promotion is off the table. In fact, she doesn't even need to come in Monday morning. It's your choice."

At eight o'clock the next morning, Felicity rang Austin's room. She hadn't slept much after Miles had stumbled upon their late-night kiss. Instead, she'd stayed up all night contemplating what to say to him the next time they talked.

She'd considered texting him—actually, she wanted to text him the minute she'd closed the door between them, wondering if Miles had called or texted or walked across the hall and pounded on Austin's door. Knowing Miles, it wasn't so far-fetched.

If Miles had started the inquisition, the last thing Austin needed was her texts pinging his phone. If Miles had been uncharacteristically silent, she didn't want to crowd Austin.

So, she'd forced herself to wait until the respectable hour of eight o'clock to ring his room phone. When he didn't answer, she called the front desk and discovered that he had already checked out.

She could've kicked herself for not texting last night. Because even if she hadn't wanted to seem desperate, she was feeling that way more and more with each hour that ticked on without word from him.

Checkout was at eleven o'clock. Felicity decided she wouldn't leave a minute earlier. She took a hot bath in the suite's garden tub. Then she took her time applying moisturizer from head to toe, styling her hair, putting on her makeup and getting dressed. She ordered room service and leisurely enjoyed the fruit plate, pastry basket and the entire pot of strong hot coffee.

She called the bellhop to assist her with her luggage and getting her car from the valet. She would not allow herself to check her phone until she was parked in her own driveway. Because by that time it was a quarter past noon. Surely, Austin would've made time to get in touch.

But there were no new texts waiting for her after she got home.

She had also imposed another moratorium on herself. Until she got home, she would not let herself fret over the fact that she had been the one who had initiated the kiss. Oh, sure, Austin had kissed her back, but what was he supposed to do?

No. She wasn't going there. Austin had definitely been into the kiss. And he had been the one who had asked her to dance the second time, the one who had suggested the drink at Sazerac and had purchased the champagne and had walked past his own room to escort her to hers. Those were not mixed signals. Those were *beacons*. Spotlight-strong beacons. And that's why she had leaned in and kissed him.

Felicity shored up her confidence. She let herself out of the car, hitched her handbag up onto her shoulder, grabbed her suitcase and the garment bag that contained the red dress that Maia had lent her for the gala. She carted her belongings onto the porch.

She had just put the key into the lock when she heard a car turn into her driveway. In the split second between hearing the sound and turning around, her heart leaped in her chest and possibility bloomed like the roses she loved.

But it was short-lived, because when she turned around, she saw that it was not Austin. It was a courier lugging a huge box up the walk.

"Felicity Schafer?" he asked.

"Yes."

"This is for you. Please sign here."

She did, and he set the large brown box inside her front door.

Who in the world would be sending her a package? Maybe it was something for graduation. That's when her heart took a second leap of faith and imagined it was from her father.

But it wasn't.

When she opened the box, there was a card, which she didn't open right away. It took a moment to figure it out, but the pieces in the box were for a greenhouse. Inside the larger note there was a piece of paper with a number for her to call to make an appointment for someone to assemble it for her.

It should've been the most wonderful moment. It should've made her happier than receiving the most fabulous piece of jewelry or the most coveted designer bag. But it didn't. Written on the note card in Austin's own handwriting was a message that broke her heart.

I'm sorry, Felicity. I crossed the line. It will never happen again. I hope Monday we can carry on as before.

This proved her theory that love was definitely real, but once acknowledged, a clock started counting down to the end. She never dreamed it would end before it had a chance to begin with Austin.

## Chapter Twelve

Austin had contemplated calling Felicity Sunday night, but he decided it would have made things worse. It would've felt too personal. As it stood, things were already personal enough. So, it was for the best that he waited to talk to her again Monday morning at the office.

He didn't like it. Not one bit, but that's the way things had to be. For her sake.

After his early-morning conversation with his dad, Austin had needed time to think and get his head together. Miles might be able to keep them apart by threatening Felicity's promotion, but his mandate wouldn't change the way he felt about her.

For the first time in a long time, he was falling in love.

He was in love with Felicity, but for her sake, there

was nothing he could do about it. He couldn't get in the way of her promotion. He had to let her have this opportunity.

He stepped off the elevator at Fortune Investments and into the hallway that led to their office. He was arriving at his usual time and he planned to act like it was any other day. If he sensed she wanted to talk about things, they could do that in his office—just as they would talk about anything on any given day.

His heart thudded as he rounded the corner and saw her sitting at her desk, typing on her computer. It thudded, then it settled into a dull ache.

"Good morning," he said.

"Good morning." She didn't look up from what she was doing.

*Okay.* Apparently, this was going to be more difficult than he'd anticipated. On both of their parts. She was wearing a red dress that managed to look sexy and all business at the same time. His need for her was a visceral ache.

And he needed to stop noticing what she was wearing. How had he done that before? Back before everything went haywire and he realized that she was the best thing that had ever happened to him. Was it any wonder that he was in love with her?

There had to be a way to work this out and the only way to do that was to level with her. Even though his father had acted like a jackass about the situation, tossing around ultimatums and mandates, Austin wouldn't betray him by telling Felicity point-blank what Miles had said after he'd found them together. He'd have to keep the conversation more general. He'd have to tell her that due to company policy, it wasn't possible for them to work together and be together.

"Do you have a moment to talk?" he asked.

She kept typing, her gaze glued to the computer monitor. For a moment, he thought she wasn't going to answer him. But then she stopped and looked up, her eyes focused on a point somewhere over his shoulder.

"Yes. I'll be in in a moment." Her tone was strictly business. He didn't blame her.

He went into his office, which was darker than usual. Normally, Felicity turned on his lights and computer before he arrived. This morning, he had to do it himself. When he did, he realized she hadn't gotten his coffee as she usually did. He didn't blame her for that either.

Austin had never expected these little niceties, but he had appreciated them. It was also quite possible that he'd taken them for granted. Just like he'd taken her for granted, even though he hadn't done it on purpose. He'd been inadvertently careless

Just like he'd been with her heart after the gala... and all the times that had led them to that moment.

After he turned on his computer, he set out for the break room. Felicity wasn't at her desk when he passed by, but she was there when he returned with two cups of coffee in hand. One for her and one for himself.

The selection of mugs in the break room was eclectic. He handed her the mug that said You Are My Sunshine and kept the one with Snoopy lying atop his red doghouse. It would've been more appropriate if he'd been in the doghouse, but close enough.

"I made the coffee myself," he said, striving for a light tone. "It may not be as good as yours."

"Thanks, Austin," she said. "I'll show you and whoever replaces me how I make it before I leave. That way you'll both know. But in the meantime, we need to talk about other things."

Austin watched her pick up her coffee cup and a piece of paper off her desk. Then they walked silently to his office together.

She sat in the same chair that she'd sat in that first day that she'd given him her letter of resignation. He'd barely had time to sit down in his chair before she handed him the paper she held.

"This is my official two weeks' notice. The first letter I gave you was a little vague. It didn't have a date for my last day, but this one does. Now that the charity ball is behind us, I can start wrapping up other projects and you can start interviewing for my replacement. Though it might have been a good idea if we had done that earlier so he or she could've shadowed me at the gala. But it is what it is." She shrugged. "I'm graduating in two weeks and one day. Which means my last day at Fortune Investments will be the day before the ceremony."

Austin frowned at the paper, reading everything she had just told him. "You're still planning on interviewing with Miles for the advertising position, aren't you?"

She took a deep breath and shook her head. "No, Austin. I don't think so. It's probably best for me to make a clean break. For us to make a clean break."

"Felicity, please don't feel like you have to bow out just because of what happened last night."

"Last night was a mistake, Austin. You as much as said so in your note. By the way, thank you for the greenhouse, but I can't keep it. I do hope you can return it. In fact, if you'll let me know where you got it, I'm happy to see that it's returned and your account is credited."

"Felicity, please don't—"

"No, Austin. I'm afraid I'm the one who needs to say *please don't*. You made your feelings perfectly clear in the note. Let's agree not to talk about it while I serve out my two weeks. I'm sure everyone will be much better off for it."

After sorting through hundreds of résumés, narrowing the field and interviewing a dozen candidates, Felicity presented the final slate to Austin, allowing him to make the ultimate choice.

Austin chose a guy named George Daughtry.

A guy.

Not that gender mattered. Though, it was strangely gratifying that Austin had selected a guy. It felt less like she'd been replaced and more like he'd chosen the right candidate for the job. Because George had the strongest credentials.

Today was George's first full day of work. It also happened to be Felicity's last day.

While George had to work out a notice at his former job, he had come by after work so that Felicity could train him. Starting Monday, he would be on his own.

Felicity was graduating tomorrow and after the party her coworkers were throwing for her at four o'clock, she would be a free woman. She'd been so busy tying up loose ends at Fortune Investments— including writing a letter to Miles Fortune. She explained that while she appreciated his being willing to consider her for an advertising position, she thought it best if she moved on.

She hadn't yet had the opportunity to send out résumés. She would have plenty of time, though, because she had plenty of savings to allow her to take several months off if she needed to. Fortune Investments had paid well enough and she had saved diligently to afford her this privilege. This was the rainy day for which she had been saving. She spent the morning cleaning out her desk, and as each minute ticked away the hours of her last day, her heart grew heavier and heavier.

She was really doing this.

This was it. When she walked out the door tonight, it would likely be the last time she entered this building that had been her home away from home for nearly half a decade.

Ever since she'd given her notice, Austin had made himself scarce. The first week he'd been legitimately out of town on a business trip to New York City that had been on the books long before they'd known Felicity would be working out her notice. This week, he'd just been spotty.

So far, her last day was no different. Austin had not been around much today, except to meet with George for a few minutes in the morning, presumably to go over next week's schedule. Felicity had left them to meet by themselves. Aside from the fact that she hadn't been invited to sit in, it was for the best. After today, she wouldn't be around to interpret for George or clarify matters for Austin.

After she carried the last box down to her car and she had returned to her desk, her intercom buzzed. It was Carla from the front desk.

"Hey, baby girl, are you ready to party?" she asked. "We have cake." She sang the words and then lowered her voice. "God, you're so lucky you're getting out of this place. Take me with you."

"I'll see you in the conference room," Felicity said, and she hung up the phone.

She glanced at Austin's dark, empty office and felt the tears well in her eyes. She blinked them away. If he wasn't even going to show up to say goodbye, she wasn't going to waste her tears on him.

She turned off her computer for the last time, stood up from her desk, pushed in her chair, hitched her purse strap up onto her shoulder and walked toward the conference room without looking back.

The conference room was crowded with what looked like all of her Fortune Investments coworkers. Even Miles and Georgia were there. When she walked in, everyone clapped. Felicity's eyes scanned the room, but she didn't see Austin.

She hated herself for it, but her heart twisted and sank. A stinging, salty, burning sense of sorrow stung the back of her throat. She could barely swallow past the lump that had lodged there. Which made it all the more important for her to keep in place the smile she'd carefully affixed on her lips. If it slipped, the rest of the facade might, too, and fall like an avalanche. That was the last thing she needed right now. At least she still had her dignity the respect of her coworkers.

Since it hadn't been a secret that she'd given Austin her notice at the beginning of the month, no one had questioned her final date of resignation. Since none of Fortune Investments' rank and file had attended the foundation charity gala, none had been the wiser to her dances with Austin and hadn't put two and two together.

So, here she was, leaving with her reputation as Ms. Together and Efficient firmly intact.

Ha! Little did they know.

She was a hot mess on the inside.

Because despite how hard she was trying not to, all she could think about now was how fast her time with Austin had run out. She'd kissed him because she loved him and she wanted to believe that maybe, as in all the fairy tales she'd read as a child, true love would break the spell. That love would last. Like in *Beauty and the Beast*.

Did that mean he was doomed to remain a beast for the rest of his life? Probably not. He'd find love eventually.

What if she hadn't kissed him...

No. She couldn't change what was already done. She had arrived at this juncture in her life for a reason. Even if she hadn't kissed him after the gala, it would've happened eventually. And it would've ended up like this. It was time she moved on.

Carla shoved a plate of cake in Felicity's hands. It

was chocolate with white icing, her favorite. Was that a coincidence or had someone known?

The only person she could think of who knew that was Austin. Because every year on her birthday, he would buy her favorite cake and bring it into the office.

That wasn't so beastly. One of his better qualities, Felicity guessed.

She ate her cake and tried to make her way around the room to speak to as many of her colleagues as she could—even Miles Fortune, who was remarkably civil and complimentary, thanking her for her hard work and dedication to Fortune Investments. He mentioned not a word about the kiss with Austin in the hallway of the Roosevelt Hotel, but neither did he offer the standard *if you want to come back, there will always be a place for you.*

Felicity's sixth sense told her that after witnessing the kiss, ol' Miles considered her a liability, and, despite her hard work and dedication, he was happy to see her go.

And it was time.

The more she thought about it, the more she realized Austin had never really been interested in her. He'd kissed her back, but that had been the alcohol talking. Then Miles had interrupted, and the rest was history.

She disposed of her cake plate and started making her way to the door when he walked in—Austin, with his sister Savannah in tow.

Her heart leaped into her throat.

"Oh, Felicity, I'm so happy to see you." Savannah

pulled her into a hug. "Austin is taking me to the airport. We wanted to stop by before we left."

"Where's Chaz?" Felicity asked.

"He went home right after the ball. I stayed and helped Mom with some things, but now it's time for me to get back. I'm so sad that you're leaving FI. Where are you going?"

"I'm graduating tomorrow, and then I'm going to take some time off."

Even though her gaze was trained on Savannah, in Felicity's peripheral vision, she could see Austin standing behind his sister. Even more, she could feel his gaze on her. She resisted for as long as she could, but finally, she glanced up at him.

He looked as bereft as she felt. If it wouldn't have caused such a scene, she would've screamed at him. *What? Dammit! What do you want from me? You're not the one who gets to stand there looking all sad. You're the one who wanted things this way.*

"Well, I hate it that you're leaving, but the time off is well deserved. I know that workaholic brother of mine thinks that working is everyone's favorite pastime." Savannah turned to include Austin in the conversation. "Someday he'll learn."

Felicity forced her smile back into place, because it felt as if it was slipping. "I don't know. I think it's his nature. But I need to go. It was great to see you, Savannah. I'm bad at goodbyes. So I'm going to walk out of here like it's any other day."

Only, if it was any other day, she would've stayed

until after everyone else was gone, rather than being the first one to leave. But this was a new beginning.

"Could you stay for just a few more minutes?" Austin asked.

Felicity blinked. She really didn't want to, but if she said no in front of Savannah, his sister would know something was wrong.

"Sure, Austin." Her voice shook a little and she hated herself for it. She took a deep breath to steady her nerves.

Thank goodness, Austin had already begun calling the room to order.

"May I have everyone's attention, please?"

The room quieted in an instant, all eyes on Austin.

"I'm not going to lie," Austin said. "I am pretty torn up today. Because what does one do when they are losing their right-hand person? No offense to you, George, but Felicity and I go way back. Sometimes I think she knows me better than I know myself."

*Oh, God, Austin, please don't do this.*

Despite the way she'd been able to hold herself together, she felt her composure starting to slip. She tried to remind herself, again, that this was all his doing. Well, not all his doing. She had been the one to initiate the kiss. But if he had wanted her to stay, he would've told her so, and things could've been quite different right now. But it was what it was, and she was not going to cry.

She didn't even hear the rest of what Austin said, but the next thing she knew, he was gesturing toward a potted rosebush that was sitting on a nearby table.

"This is for the greenhouse that I had installed in your backyard today."

"What?" Maia was supposed to let a courier into Felicity's house today, so he could pick up the greenhouse to return it. Apparently, Maia had been working with Austin behind the scenes.

There was no need to make a scene. She would assess the situation when she got home, but in her gut, she knew that if the greenhouse had already been installed, there was probably no sending it back. The only thing she could do was be gracious as Austin gestured toward the rosebush and leaned in for a kiss on the cheek.

"I don't know what I'm going to do without you," he whispered as everyone else in the room applauded.

"I'm sure you will be fine, Austin. You'll be just fine."

"What's going on?" Savannah asked after she and Austin were in the car and on the way to the airport.

"Do you mean right in this moment, or with life in general?" Austin asked her, though he knew exactly what she meant.

"Don't be a smart-ass. You know what I'm talking about."

Austin slanted a glance at his sister, trying to figure out the best way to skirt the subject. He did not want to talk about it right now.

"Eyes on the road, buddy. Drive and talk."

He was silent for a few beats too long.

"Why is Felicity quitting? Tell me the real reason."

"She is graduating with her MBA tomorrow. She's

overqualified to be my handmaiden. It's time she moved on."

Savannah was quiet in that way people were when they weren't buying what you were trying to sell.

"I mean, think about it," he tried, desperately needing to fill the skeptical silence. "It would be a colossal waste of her time, talent and energy if she used that expensive education working as anybody's assistant. Even mine. Especially mine."

"And what happened to the advertising director position Dad was supposedly creating for her? It sounded like a dream job for someone in her position. It sounded like Miles was pretty gung ho about it. He was going to have her work with Georgia and between the two of them—"

"I know that. It didn't work out." He didn't mean to growl.

"It didn't work out for who?"

"I don't know. You'll have to ask Dad. No. Don't ask Dad."

"Well, I am going to ask Dad. In fact, I'll call him right now, if you don't tell me what's really going on."

Austin stared ahead at the ribbon of highway that stretched out in front of him. There was remarkably light traffic for a Friday evening. His heart felt very heavy as he relayed everything that had transpired between Felicity and him to his sister.

When he finished, she sat there for a moment without saying anything. Then he wished she would've remained silent because all she said was, "You're an idiot. I love you, but you're still an idiot."

"Yeah, I suppose I am. But that's not going to change anything. It's a whole hell of a lot more complicated than that."

"What are you talking about? You are in complete control of the situation. You are the one who is keeping the two of you apart. My God, Austin, sometimes you are your own worst enemy. Don't you see it?"

"Obviously not." His voice was monotone, because if he didn't keep it calm and level, he really felt like he was going to lose it. Not on his sister, but just on life in general.

The past two weeks he had been mad at the world because of the catch-22 he had found himself in. "If I would've defied company policy and continued to pursue the relationship, she not only would've lost the advertising job, but Miles probably would've fired us both. Then irony of ironies, she ended up turning the job down anyway."

"So…" Savannah dragged out the word. "I don't get it. What's keeping you apart now? The minute Felicity walked out that door, she was no longer a Fortune Investments employee. What's stopping you now?"

*Nothing.*

*Everything.*

Austin's head swam, and his aching heart thudded in his chest.

"She doesn't even want to talk to me. I screwed it up as I always do with things like this. It's over. It's done."

"It never even started, Austin, because you didn't give it a chance. Felicity is not Kelly. And you're letting Kelly rob you of a whole lot more than money if you let the ghost of your relationship come between you and Felicity."

Essentially, Felicity had said the same thing.

"Anyone who knows the two of you can see as plain as day that she is in love with you. And I know you and I can see that you are in love with her. You're just too big of an idiot to get out of your own way.

"Actually, let me rephrase that—you're too scared because of how things went down with your ex-wife to let things bloom with Felicity. You *will* be an idiot if you don't go after her and let her walk away. Austin, don't let her walk away. You have used work as an excuse for too long. You've been hiding behind the one mistake you made when you were twenty-five years old. It's time that you forgive yourself, quit punishing yourself. Put the past behind you and start living the life you deserve."

Sometimes it just took somebody you loved and trusted to hold up a mirror in front of your face, so you could see exactly how big of a dolt you were being and how much you stood to lose. Tonight, Savannah had held up that mirror.

Austin could feel the feelings she was talking about. He knew they were there living inside him, trapped in his heart, but he couldn't identify them to save his life. Not until his little sister had shone the spotlight on everything and made him realize he had to face his fears.

Thank God, Austin thought. Thank God he had snapped out of it before it was too late. If it wasn't too late already. He'd never know unless he tried.

On the drive home, after he'd dropped Savannah off at the airport, everything crystallized. Why was he willing to watch the best thing that had ever happened to him walk out of his life forever, without at least trying to save the relationship?

Felicity was worth it.

The two of them together—they were worth it.

They deserved a fighting chance. He didn't know if she felt the same way, but he would be an idiot if he didn't at least do what he could to let her know how he felt. The best way to start was by telling her exactly how he felt about her. He was in love with her. This wasn't just a passing whim. These feelings had been building for nearly five years. He owed it to himself and to her and to their future to let her know how he felt, even if it meant risking her rejecting him and telling him she didn't feel the same way.

On the drive home, an idea brewed. A big gesture. It might very well backfire in his face. Felicity might look at him and tell him to go to hell. But he had to do it. He had to chance it. Because she was the love of his life.

Felicity woke the morning of her graduation feeling empty and overcome by a sense of gray ennui. Maybe it was mental exhaustion after everything she had endured the past two weeks. Actually, going back even further than that—the whole buildup to the charity gala, the buildup and eventual letdown with Austin. The final two weeks at Fortune Investments spent avoiding each other in an awkward dance of pretending. Or, at least, pretending on her part. Then, the grand finale when she thought Austin would be a no-show at her going away party, and true to form, then Austin had changed everything, coming through the door at the very last minute.

But now, she was free. She wouldn't have to ride that roller coaster any longer. The messed-up thing about it was she was sad. She had worked so damn hard to get to this day, to get her MBA, which was supposed to set her free, but now more than ever she felt as if it had been the instrument of her demise.

She got out of bed, shuffled into the kitchen and poured herself a cup of coffee that had autobrewed, knowing that she was being overly dramatic. The MBA hadn't been the cause of her demise. What happened between her and Austin had been inevitable and so had their parting of ways. This was like the day after an accident where she had been banged up. She didn't realize how badly her pride had been wounded until now; it had suffered a beating. Every day from here on out, she would get stronger and feel better. The first thing she had to do was make sure she held her head high and kept a positive outlook.

She had just finished showering and getting dressed when Maia knocked on her door. Her arms were loaded down with makeup and hair implements.

"Good morning, graduation girl. On a special day like this, I come to you. Is Beauty ready for the royal treatment?"

*Ahh*, Maia. What would she do without her friend? Even if she did sometimes take matters into her own hands, like she did with the greenhouse. Last night, when she had gotten home, she had scolded Maia for being in cahoots with Austin about the greenhouse, but all Mira had said was, "It's a nice present. Just be gracious. Or if you don't want it, I'll take it. I don't know what I'll do with it, because you're the woman with the green thumb, but you can't give it back now."

She was right. After mulling it over for a couple of hours, Felicity decided there was a lesson in it. In these new days of freedom, she needed to free her mind of the structure and the worry that had gotten her nowhere.

So, she relaxed with a mimosa from the pitcher that Maia had mixed. The friends chatted away about everything and nothing as Maia fixed Felicity's hair and makeup for her big day.

Three hours later, Felicity had her diploma cover in hand and she walked out into the audience of the auditorium to meet her mother and Maia who had come to cheer her on.

Her mother stood there with Maia, who held a bunch of sunflowers bound by a beautiful green ribbon in one arm like a runner-up in a beauty pageant and a bouquet of balloons in the other. She looked as if she might float away if a big gust of wind happened to blow through. Alas, they were indoors so there was no chance of that.

By this time, the auditorium had started to empty out. The people who lingered were gathered in small knots, congratulating their graduates with high fives, hugs and gifts. As her mother held out her arms and gathered Felicity to her, murmuring about how proud she was of her, Felicity reminded herself of how lucky she was to have the love and support of these two wonderful women. That love was guaranteed to last. It wouldn't float away like balloons on a storm. She had so much to be grateful for, and soon this empty feeling would dissipate. She would fill it with new adventures and she would feel like herself again. Eventually.

No, not like herself, maybe a better version of herself? Actually, right now, she would settle for feeling like herself again, because when she put everything else aside, that wasn't a bad thing.

Then she saw him. He was standing a few rows back holding a bouquet of roses. At first, she thought her mind had conjured the vision, that her eyes were playing tricks on her. Because ever since the kiss—the kiss that had changed her from the inside out—Austin Fortune had been living in the back of her mind. He had taken up residence in the hollowed-out place in her heart that felt like it would never again be whole because he held her heart in his hands.

But Felicity blinked, shook her head, and he was still there. He lifted his hand, tentatively as she pulled out of her mother's embrace. Almost in unison, Maia and her mom turned to see who she was looking at.

"Oh!" the two women said.

"Maia, is that who I think it is?" Mom asked in a stage whisper.

"Yes, it is. You know, I need to visit the ladies room. Who wants to come with me?"

Felicity's mother raised her hand. "I do."

The women hadn't taken two steps before Felicity saw them motion to Austin to approach, and then, as they walked away, they were chattering on about how good-looking he was and what a gorgeous couple he and Felicity made. If Felicity had been in her right mind, she might have turned and walked away with her mom and Maia, but she was rooted to the spot.

"Congratulations," Austin said. He handed her the blood red roses. There had to be at least five dozen. The bouquet was almost unwieldy, but it was breathtakingly beautiful. Austin shoved his hands in his back pockets. "I hope you don't mind me being here, but your graduation was on my calendar and…and I had some things to tell you. Don't worry, I'm not here to try to convince you to come back to work. If you want to get a new job, I just want you to be happy."

He pulled one hand out of his pocket and raked it through his hair and muttered a choice word under his breath. "And I am making the biggest mess out of this. It's so damn hard for me to admit my feelings, because for the longest time I didn't believe in true love. I was convinced it was a myth.

"But then you came along, and you made me a believer. Not that love was a myth. You made me believe in love. What I'm trying to say in my clumsy way is I'm in love with you, Felicity. I've probably been in love with you since the moment I first saw you. There's a dozen roses for every year we've known each other. And if you'll give me a chance, I'd like the opportunity to give you many more dozen roses in the years to come. Can we start over, or better yet, pick up where we left off in the hallway of the Roosevelt and—?"

Felicity didn't let him finish. She shifted the bouquet to one arm and threw her other arm around him, planting a kiss on his lips that left no doubt where she wanted them to go next.

When they finally came up for air, she said, "Austin Fortune, you're still a piece of work, but you're my piece of work and I wouldn't have it any other way. I love you so much."

At the sound of clapping and Maia's whoops, Felicity turned around to see her mother and her friend beaming at them. As Austin put his arm around her, Felicity shifted the bouquet of roses from one arm to another. A few petals floated to the ground.

Beauty had finally tamed the Beast.

Afterward, Austin took Felicity, her mother and Maia to Commander's Palace for a celebratory dinner. It was important for Felicity to bask in her accomplishments, surrounded by the people who loved her. Austin was so happy to be part of the celebration, but he would've been lying if he didn't admit, the entire time, all he wanted was for the two of them to be alone.

He'd waited years for her—even if he hadn't been fully cognizant of that fact until a few weeks ago.

Now, they sat in his living room. The only question was, where did they go from here? He handed her a glass of champagne. As he lowered himself onto the couch next to her, she smiled and gave her head a quick shake.

"What's wrong?" he asked.

"Nothing." She squeezed her eyes shut and smiled. "This is dumb, but I just realized this is the first time that I've been to your home and it hasn't been about business."

Austin searched her eyes, looking for a clue as to how she felt about being there. Was it too much? Was she putting on the breaks? He knew what he wanted. He wanted Felicity and not just for the short-term. But he needed to make sure she wanted the same thing.

"I don't want you to be uncomfortable?" he asked. "If you are, we can take things slowly—"

Suddenly, her lips were on his and her arms were around his neck. She claimed his lips in a kiss that seared his soul. She slid her hands into in his hair, pulling him closer. He responded by taking the champagne flute from her hand and setting it on the table. He wrapped his arms around her and pulled her in tight, as if he'd never let her go. Every inch of her body was pressed against his. He lost himself in the heated tenderness of that kiss.

Once, the mere thought of caring for someone that much scared him, but no more. He'd already passed the point of no return. There was no denying the truth. He'd fallen. And hard.

He was in love with Felicity.

He pulled back and placed his hands on either side of her cheeks. "I love you," he whispered, looking into her eyes, savoring the depth of their connection.

"I love you, too."

Those perfect words passed over her perfect lips and wrapped around his heart, touching him in places where he thought he would never be able to feel anything again. Places he once thought were dead, he now knew were very much alive.

Desire grew as he held her and tasted her. In response his own body swelled and hardened. He loved the feel of her curves, sexy and supple to his touch. When he dropped his hands to her hips and pulled her onto his lap, she arched against him fueling his desire.

"I want you," she murmured breathlessly.

He wanted to show her exactly how much he ached for her. Instead of using words, he stood and picked her up, carrying her to the bedroom.

The anticipation of their lovemaking sent a shudder wracking his whole body. He needed her naked so that he could bury himself inside of her. She wanted the same thing, because when he set her on the bed, she began to unbuckle the button on his pants, slid down the zipper and freed them of one of the barriers that stood between them. He shrugged off his shirt, unashamed of his nakedness.

Wanting to permanently imprint her on his senses, he deliberately slowed down, undoing each button of her blouse. Pushing it away, he unhooked the front clasp on her bra. As he freed her breasts, she lay back on the bed, and he lowered himself next to her. In turn, his mouth worshipped each one until she cried out in pleasure. Then, when he was sure she was ready, he stripped off her trousers and panties.

As they lay together—skin to skin, soul to soul— once again, he purposely slowed down, taking a moment to savor the way she looked and commit to memory the beauty of her body.

This was the Felicity he loved.

And then they were reaching for each other and touching everywhere, a tangle of arms and legs. He kissed her deeply—tongues thrusting, hands exploring, teeth nipping, bodies moving together in the most sensual pas de deux. Austin wasn't cognizant of space or time, he was only aware of her—the smell of her, the taste of her, the feel of her and the realization that he could not bear to spend another day—or night—in this world without her.

His heart, body and soul belonged to her.

He needed to make her his.

"Now," she whispered, her breath hot on his neck. And he buried himself deep inside her.

As they lay together, spent and glowing, Felicity snuggled deeper into the crook of Austin's arm—a place where she fit so perfectly it felt as if it had been made for her. She turned her cheek and nuzzled his chest, breathing in the scent of him—that delicious smell of cedar, coffee and leather. She breathed in deeply and melted a little more with the heat of his body.

But he moved, propping himself up on his elbow. He smoothed an errant lock of hair off her forehead, kissed the skin he'd just uncovered.

"I could get used to this," he said.

She smiled up at him. "I already have."

He pulled her into his arms and kissed her. Then he held her so close she could hear his heart beat. For the first time in ages, she felt safe and things felt right. She knew she was exactly where she belonged. Together, they completed each other.

Together, they were whole.

## Epilogue

Thanksgiving at Miles and Sarah's was almost over-whelming, in the very best, most thrilling way. The whole family was there—all of Austin's siblings along with their spouses and significant others.

Miles and Sarah had graciously welcomed Felicity's mother and Maia to the festivities. Over the months, Felicity had grown quite fond of Miles and Sarah and Austin's huge, boisterous family.

After Miles offered Felicity the advertising direc-tor position, he had made a special exception to the Fortune Investments' no fraternizing policy, allowing Austin and Felicity to have the best of both worlds. Be-cause of that, she was regularly included in the family's infamous dinners. Sometimes those could get a little lively with all of the big Fortune opinions.

After all the years of growing up as an only child, with it just being Felicity and her mother, the Fortunes were the big, warm family she never knew she had always wanted.

This Thanksgiving Day also held another special meaning. Felicity and Austin had officially been together for six months. Six months and they were getting stronger every day. Finally, she had let go of the notion that love had an expiration date. Crushes and flights of fancy might expire, but true love knew no end.

Today, as the family sat around the big dining room table, the waitstaff that Sarah had hired effortlessly facilitated the holiday meal, including serving the delicious-looking desserts on display on the antique buffet.

The server had poured champagne to go with the pumpkin pie. It was a combination that Felicity and her mother had never enjoyed during their small celebrations—they usually paired coffee with pie—but she was constantly learning new things from this family.

The servers were still plating slices of pie when Austin stood and began gently pinging the side of his crystal champagne flute with a sterling silver knife.

"I am so happy we could all be together this holiday. As I look around the table, I realize how much we have to be thankful for. We are truly blessed. Our family is happy and healthy and we're all together. That's why I couldn't think of a better time to do this."

Felicity saw Austin exchange knowing glances with his father and then her mother.

"Six months ago today, I finally came to my senses and took a chance on confessing my love to Felicity. Ever since that day, I've never looked back. That was, without a doubt, the smartest move I've ever made in my life. Until today."

Little pinpricks of dawning skittered up and down Felicity's body. The subsequent events unfolded in a surreal sort of slow motion: Austin turned toward her; he took her hand; he lowered himself down on one knee; he reached into his pocket with his free hand and pulled out a small light blue jewelry box. Somehow, he managed to open it with one hand, revealing a stunning sparkler of an oval diamond.

"Felicity Schafer, you are the woman who finally made me believe in love. Will you make me the happiest man in the world and be my wife?"

The events may have happened in slow motion, but Austin's words were crystal clear and so was her instantaneous response. "Yes!"

The room erupted into raucous applause. Miles Fortune raised his glass. "To Austin and Felicity. To family, old and new. Happy Thanksgiving and many, many years of love and happiness."

\* \* \* \* \*

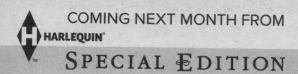

# COMING NEXT MONTH FROM
# HARLEQUIN°
## SPECIAL EDITION

### Available May 21, 2019

### #2695 A FORTUNE'S TEXAS REUNION
*The Fortunes of Texas: The Lost Fortunes* • by Allison Leigh
Georgia Fortune is excited to travel to small-town Texas for a family reunion—until her car breaks down! Luckily, Sheriff Paxton Price comes to the rescue and they quickly realize the attraction between them is mutual! The only question is—can it last?

### #2696 THE MAVERICK'S SUMMER SWEETHEART
*Montana Mavericks* • by Stacy Connelly
Gemma Chapman is on her honeymoon—alone! But when she befriends a little girl staying at the same hotel, Gemma suddenly finds herself spending lots of time with the girl's father: Hank, a rough-around-the-edges cowboy who might be able to give her the feeling of belonging she's always craved.

### #2697 THE COWBOY'S SECRET FAMILY
*Rocking Chair Rodeo* • by Judy Duarte
Miranda Contreras is back and she has her daughter in tow. The daughter Matt Grimes didn't know about. But after fleeing a broken engagement, Miranda needs somewhere to go and her hometown is her best bet, even if it puts all her secrets in danger of coming to light!

### #2698 IT STARTED WITH A PREGNANCY
*Furever Yours* • by Christy Jeffries
Animal rescue director Rebekah Taylor isn't a pet person—or the family type. But now she's pregnant and a newbie parent to an adventure-loving stray dog nobody can catch, kind of like Grant Whitaker, her baby's father. Except he's sticking around. Can Grant persuade Rebekah to trust in him?

### #2699 HAVING THE SOLDIER'S BABY
*The Parent Portal* • by Tara Taylor Quinn
Emily and Winston Hannigan had a fairy-tale romance until he died for his country. So when Winston arrives on her doorstep very much alive after two years, Emily's overjoyed. Winston may have survived the unthinkable but he believes he doesn't deserve Emily—or their unborn child.

### #2700 FOR THEIR CHILD'S SAKE
*Return to Stonerock* • by Jules Bennett
Two years ago, Sam Bailey lost the two people who mattered most. Now his daughter needs him. Despite their still-powerful attraction, Tara isn't ready to trust her estranged husband. But Sam is taking this chance to fight for their future, to redeem himself in Tara's eyes—so they can be a family again.

---

**YOU CAN FIND MORE INFORMATION ON UPCOMING HARLEQUIN° TITLES, FREE EXCERPTS AND MORE AT WWW.HARLEQUIN.COM.**

HSECNM0519

# Get 4 FREE REWARDS!

### We'll send you 2 FREE Books plus 2 FREE Mystery Gifts.

**Harlequin® Special Edition** books feature heroines finding the balance between their work life and personal life on the way to finding true love.

FREE Value Over $20

---

When Matt looked up, she offered him a shy smile. "Like
I said, I'm sorry. I should have told you that you were a
father."

"You've got that right."

"I've made mistakes, but Emily isn't one of them.
She's a great kid. So for now, let's focus on her."

"All right." Matt uncrossed his arms and raked a hand
through his hair. "But just for the record, I would've done
anything in my power to take care of you and Emily."

"I know." And that was why she'd walked away from
him. Matt would have stood up to her father, challenged
his threat, only to be knocked to his knees—and worse.

No, leaving town and cutting all ties with Matt was the
only thing she could've done to protect him.

As she stood in the room where their daughter was conceived, as she studied the only man she'd ever loved, the memories crept up on her…the old feelings, too.

When she was sixteen, there'd been something about the fun-loving nineteen-year-old cowboy that had drawn her attention. And whatever it was continued to tug at her now. But she shook it off. Too many years had passed; too many tears had been shed.

Besides, an unwed single mother who was expecting another man's baby wouldn't stand a chance with a champion bull rider who had his choice of pretty cowgirls. And she'd best not forget that.

"Aw, hell," Matt said, as he ran a hand through his hair again and blew out a weary sigh. "Maybe you did Emily a favor by leaving when you did. Who knows what kind of father I would have made back then. Or even now."

*Don't miss*
The Cowboy's Secret Family *by Judy Duarte,*
*available June 2019 wherever*
*Harlequin® Special Edition books and ebooks are sold.*

www.Harlequin.com

Looking for more satisfying love stories
with community and family at their core?

Check out **Harlequin®** Special Edition
and **Love Inspired®** books!

 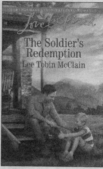

**New books available every month!**

---

**CONNECT WITH US AT:**

Facebook.com/groups/HarlequinConnection

 Facebook.com/HarlequinBooks

Twitter.com/HarlequinBooks

Instagram.com/HarlequinBooks

Pinterest.com/HarlequinBooks

ReaderService.com

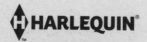 **HARLEQUIN®**

**ROMANCE WHEN
YOU NEED IT**

HFGENRE2018

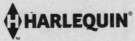

# *Love Harlequin romance?*

## DISCOVER.

Be the first to find out about promotions, news and exclusive content!

**f** Facebook.com/HarlequinBooks

**t** Twitter.com/HarlequinBooks

**o** Instagram.com/HarlequinBooks

**p** Pinterest.com/HarlequinBooks

ReaderService.com

## EXPLORE.

Sign up for the Harlequin e-newsletter and download a free book from any series at **TryHarlequin.com.**

## CONNECT.

Join our Harlequin community to share your thoughts and connect with other romance readers!
**Facebook.com/groups/HarlequinConnection**

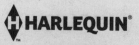

**H HARLEQUIN®**

**ROMANCE WHEN YOU NEED IT**